EL CHUPACABRAS

EL CHUPACABRAS

Trail of the Goatsucker

Lloyd S. Wagner
Illustrated by Natalie Hoffner
Cover Illustration by Ian Wagner & Natalie
Hoffner

iUniverse, Inc.
New York Lincoln Shanghai

El Chupacabras
Trail of the Goatsucker

iUniverse, Inc.

For information address:
iUniverse, Inc.
2021 Pine Lake Road, Suite 100
Lincoln, NE 68512
www.iuniverse.com

ISBN: 0-595-33315-X (pbk)
ISBN: 0-595-66839-9 (cloth)

Printed in the United States of America

To Cindy, Ian and Lloyd Jr.;
For their faith, inspiration and unflagging support.
Thank you.

To Mary Jones,
who loves the children.
You are sadly missed.

And Olivia Anne.

And thank you to:
Ken Vose, teacher and friend, Robert Connolly, Tim Murray, Bryan Shabrowski,
all those that helped, all those that listened and all those who encouraged me.

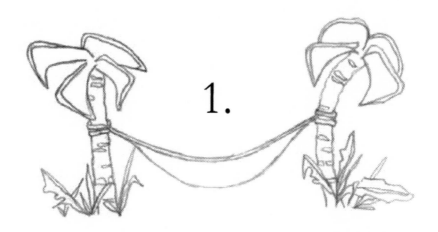

1.

"El Chupacabras"

Tyler and Tommy Oliver stared at the bearded stranger sitting beside them. Clearly he was speaking to them but they were too surprised to answer.

The man had already been seated when the boys and their family boarded the jet to begin their vacation. Since greeting them with a quiet "Hola" and a weak smile he had remained hidden behind a newspaper for most of the trip.

"El Chupacabras," the man said again, nodding and smiling.

Pointing at the drawing in Tommy's hand he explained, "Where I come from it is known as El Chupacabras."

The drawing was one of Tyler's. It pictured a black creature, outlined in yellow, with fangs, spikes on its head and huge red eyes with no pupils.

Tommy, who was never shy, spoke up.

"It's a goatsucker."

That is what Tyler called it and as far as Tommy was concerned his older brother was always right. The man rubbed his beard and thought for a moment.

"This goatsucker, what does it do?" he asked looking at Tyler.

Self-consciously, Tyler shrugged and spoke quietly.

"I don't know. They're like a monster vampire."

"Si," said the man. "Your goatsucker, we call it El Chupacabras."

"Oh," said Tyler, surprised to meet an adult who knew of it. He had heard of it from his friends at school and had drawn his picture based on what they had told him. He thought for a moment then spoke.

"El chupa...?"

"Chup—a—cabras," the stranger said slowly.

Tyler repeated the word and the man nodded his approval. Tommy looked at him.

"Do they really suck the blood from animals?" he asked.

"Si," the stranger answered, "from their heads." With a mischievous smile he added, "Not only from animals my friend."

"Cool," said Tommy.

"Have you ever seen one?" asked Tyler.

"No," said the stranger, "but I have seen pictures, even a videotape of one. It was crossing a road during a storm. It was all hunched over but you could tell, you could see what it was."

"Yeah," Tyler agreed excitedly, "My friend Chris saw that too. He's the one who told me about goatsuckers."

"El Chupacabras," the man corrected.

"El Chupacabras," Tyler agreed.

"Where are you from?" he asked.

The stranger looked out the window of the airplane.

"From there," he said, pointing. "Puerto Rico."

Tyler and Tommy looked. There was an island to be seen. It sat in the sea like a green gem in a silver setting.

Across the aisle nine-year-old Paige Oliver leaned forward, listening to ten-year-old Tyler and seven-year-old Tommy talking to the stranger seated next to them. She sat between her mother Judy and Tom Oliver. Tom and Judy had recently married which made him her stepfather and the boys her stepbrothers. Paige wasn't used to living with other children, especially boys. Suddenly having two brothers wasn't easy.

Paige looked to her mother, who was also listening to the boys. She rolled her eyes and sighed.

"Boys," her mother said and shrugged. "They love that creepy stuff."

"I know," Paige agreed.

"Is that all?" her mother asked.

Paige shrugged again. "I don't know. Sometimes it seems like they don't want me around."

"Remember honey, for eight years it's been just them. Now here you are," her mother explained, as she had many times before. "It's going to take a little time."

"It's been three months," Paige complained, "I'm tired of trying."

"Stop trying and just be yourself," Judy suggested. Looking at Paige she sighed. "Don't worry, this vacation will help."

"Will there be other children there," Paige asked, "Just in case."

Tom had been listening to them. He looked at Paige.

"Do you want me to talk to the boys?"

"No," Paige answered, shaking her head. Looking for something to read she pulled a travel magazine from the pocket in front of her. Leafing through it she stopped at a map.

Tom leaned over and pointed to their vacation destination on the map. Belize. It was tucked in a little corner below Mexico. It looked like a tiny place.

Paige read the description aloud.

"Belize. A Caribbean *backwater* once a favorite haunt of pirates, now a popular destination for scuba diving and sport fishing. Belize is noted for its *barrier reef*, the longest in the *western hemisphere*, its rain forest and an abundance of *Mayan* ruins."

"That doesn't sound bad," her mother said.

"Just like Disney," Paige answered moodily. That was where she had wanted to go.

Before Tyler and Tommy could further question their new *acquaintance* about goatsuckers they were landing at Puerto Rico airport. This busy airport bustled with people from many places speaking many different languages. There were French-speaking women from Haiti wearing bright sunny dresses and Spanish speaking men from Mexico, German-speaking tourists on their way to St. Lucia and men with *dreadlocks* who spoke English with an accent that tickled Tommy's ears. They were from Jamaica.

From Puerto Rico the Olivers went on a smaller plane to Belize City. There the airport was much smaller—just one big building really—and not busy at all. Here the people were relaxed. They took their time, laughing and joking while they did what they had to do.

From Belize City they had one more flight. This time they were on a small propeller driven plane. Tommy got to sit up front, right next to the pilot!

"Don't touch a thing Fingers," his father warned. His father often called him that because he was always getting into things.

With a roar—and a bump or two—the small plane took off. The children thought it was cool but Judy was nervous. This was already more adventure than she was used to.

In minutes they were over the water, following a chain of small *key islands* to where they would be staying. They flew low enough to see the bright beaches and palm trees. The water was so pure that they could see schools of fish like silver shadows and manta rays moving like big birds in the water. When Paige saw a shark, the pilot circled around it so that all could see.

This time when they landed the airport was even smaller. There wasn't even a building, just a bench to sit on!

The final leg of their journey was by water taxi. There on those small islands, where there are no roads, people travel back and forth by boat and those boats are called water taxis. Wearing their life vests Tommy, Tyler and Paige sat in the *bow*. Their parents sat in the *stern* close to the man who ran the boat.

The boat left the dock, slowly passing a beachfront hotel and several homes with white washed walls and red tile roofs.

As soon as they had left these buildings behind they began racing across the water. Riding in the bow, the children loved the way the boat slapped the water, sending a spray of water over their heads each time. In the back Tom held his hat on. Judy's hair was a marvelous mess.

The shore they passed was mostly *mangrove* and palm trees, and looked like a jungle. Occasionally, they passed a beach, or a small home. Paige wondered what it would be like to live there.

There weren't any waves on shore. Instead, the waves were out on the sea, on the other side of the boat.

Tom yelled over the roar of the engine.

"See those waves out there."

He pointed to the waves out on the sea.

"That's where the barrier reef is. That's where we will snorkel."

"Cool," Paige said to Tyler and Tommy, joining in their excitement.

She settled into her seat, enjoying the ride. Watching some local children swimming she thought, "Maybe this won't be too bad."

By now their Mom and Dad were talking to the man who was piloting the boat. Seeing some modern buildings Tom pointed and asked, "Is that where we are staying?"

"No sir," the man said seriously. "That is Rattan. It is a resort that never opened."

Partially hidden by palm trees the buildings looked mysterious. The largest was shaped like a squat pyramid and the front of it looked like it was made of glass. Between the building and the water there was a low wall and wide steps leading to an unfinished dock.

"So it just sits there?"

"Si. Until the jungle takes it back," the man answered. Then he spoke a little more quietly. "They say smugglers and such people use it at night. It is not a good place."

Not long after passing Rattan, the water taxi slowed.
They were there!

2.

Ahead a long dock came into view, along with some simple buildings and a large white boat.

As the boat drew closer the children pointed to shore. The dock was marked with flags that snapped in the breeze. The buildings were white, with orange tile roofs, shaded by tall coconut palms.

"Check it out," said Tyler, looking at the large boat.

"Cool," said Tommy, spotting *hammocks* hung under palm trees.

"Mom," Paige called out, "look at the little houses!" She pointed to the resort's many *cabanas*. They were where the guests stayed.

Paige's mom smiled and nodded. She was glad they were excited. She was even more glad that their *trek* was over—especially the boat ride.

The Olivers could see a man waiting for them. Slowing to a stop the boat bumped up against the wood pilings of the dock. Tyler, Paige and Tommy climbed out as soon as it was tied fast. Tom quickly followed.

Speaking with a hint of a French accent the man greeted Tom.

"Mr. Oliver," he said courteously, "I am Reaux, the manager. We spoke on the phone."

Tyler looked at him curiously. Reaux was a small black man with a narrow, serious face. His hair was cut short, so short he almost looked bald. At first, when he looked at the children, Reaux didn't seem pleased to see them. When he finally did smile it was so broad, and his teeth so bright, that it startled Tyler.

Shaking his hand Tom said, "Mr. Reaux, nice to meet you."

"Please, just Reaux. We are relaxed here."

"Fine, call me Tom. And this is Tyler, Paige and Tom Junior."

"Call me Tommy," Tommy chimed.

"Welcome to Journey's End," Reaux said with a bow to Tommy, "It is a pleasure to meet you."

"Hello," said Paige.

Tyler, who was often the shyest of the three, only nodded.

While they spoke Paige's mom was being helped out of the boat. Relieved to finally be standing on something solid she smiled.

"Hello."

"You must be Mrs. Oliver," Reaux said to her.

Tom introduced his wife then turned to the children.

"Why don't you guys go ahead and look around while we check in," he suggested.

Before the words were out of his mouth Tyler, Paige and Tommy were running down the dock toward the sandy shore.

"Don't go far," Judy called after them.

"There isn't far to go," Reaux assured her, "This is a very small island."

Paige slowed at the end of the dock. Up the beach a bit a girl stood watching her. Paige looked back at her for a moment then ran off to join the boys exploring.

Journey's End—the resort where they were staying—sat on a small beach near the end of this particular key island. Tall palm trees shaded everything. When the wind blew the long drooping leaves rustled and sounded like people whispering.

There was a restaurant with tables outside on a deck looking out to the water. Scattered among the palms behind the restaurant were the cabanas. These were arranged in groups of six or eight, each group around a courtyard. In the court-yards were trees and tropical flowers, hammocks and chairs. Paths wound through the resort, going from one group of cabanas to the next.

One of these paths led to the pool. At one end of the pool was a counter almost level with the water and seats in the pool. You could get a drink without leaving the pool!

Beyond the pool was the other side of the island. Here the path led into the tropical forest. The children stopped there and made their way back to the beach.

Along the way Tommy found a coconut and carried it with him. Shaking it he could hear the milk inside. Sitting in the sand under some palm trees he contem-plated the hard fruit searching its brown husk for some opening.

In the meantime, Tyler climbed along the trunk of a palm tree that had grown horizontally out over the sand. When he was over Tommy he lie on his belly with his arms and legs dangling over his brother's head.

Tommy looked up at him.

"How do you open a coconut?"

"I don't know," Tyler answered.

He wasn't interested in the coconut. He was watching Paige, who was at the water's edge near the fishing boat. As he lay there a woman and boy came out onto the boat's deck. Speaking in Spanish, the woman gave the boy some instruc-tions. The boy began hosing down the boat.

Tyler swung down off the tree and walked over to Paige. "What are you doing?"

"Watch," said Paige, anxious to share a discovery she had made. "When you step on the wet sand all these little baby crabs run out."

Tyler split his attention between Paige and the boy on the boat.

"Look. See them?"

When Tyler didn't answer Paige followed his gaze to the boat.

"There was a girl on the beach before too," she said. "She's gone now."

Before long their father came to get them. He found Tommy sitting in the sand.

"Coconut," Tommy said in one of his many silly voices. He held it up to show his father.

"Yes it is," Tom said. He called to Tyler and Paige. "Come on you two, the rooms are ready."

As they walked away from the water the boy on the boat watched them. Tommy carried his coconut with him.

They went to a group of six cabanas. Coming into the courtyard Paige spotted their luggage on a cart in front of a cabana. They hadn't seen their bags since the airport in Philadelphia.

"Is that our house?" Paige asked.

When Tom just shrugged she ran ahead to the cabana.

"Did you like the fishing boat?" Tom asked the boys.

Tyler was quick to answer. "Yeah, that's bigger than any fishing boat I've ever seen."

"Do you want to go fishing?"

"For big fish?" Tyler asked eagerly. He loved to do anything with his father.

"Big fish," his father said smiling. "We're going to catch some big fish buddy."

Paige was already in the cabana with her mother when Tyler and Tommy came in. It was no different than big hotel room. There was the bed, a chair, a table and dressers and a bathroom. It was very nice but it really was just a big room. Tom followed the boys in. He was carrying some bags and looked about for a place to set them. Looking at the bed he said, "Hey, get that dirty coconut off my bed."

"Ssshhh," teased Tommy, "It's asleep."

"Speaking of beds," Paige said, unable to contain her excitement.

"Hey, there's only one bed," Tyler noticed.

Tommy laughed and pointed to his parents.

"Where are you going to sleep?"

"We go next door," Paige blurted out. "We get our own house."

"We do?" the boys exclaimed. "Lets' go!"

They headed to the door but Tom stopped them.

"Hold up. I'm going to tell you three a few things." Looking at them sternly he spoke slowly and clearly.

"First, no fighting. Second, you keep it neat—better than your rooms at home. Okay? And when it is time to go to sleep you go to sleep. Right Tyler?"

"Yes," said Tyler who liked to stay up late.

Satisfied that they understood the rules Judy handed a plastic card to Paige.

"Okay, here is your key. We have the other one. Go open your room and take your bags in. I'll be over in a minute to help you unpack."

The three of them ran out the door, turning to the left. Tom yelled after them, "The other one."

Laughing all the way, Tyler, Paige and Tommy ran past the door going in the other direction. Seeing them laughing together Tom turned to Judy and said, "It's a good idea."

Just then Tommy ran back in, scooping his coconut up off the bed. Without a word he ran back out.

"We'll see," Judy said. "We'll see."

That night they ate dinner on the deck enjoying the cool breeze that came once the sun had set. Then they went swimming. Though tired from traveling all day the warm water felt good and the quiet was relaxing. It was very quiet.

Tyler, Paige and Tommy swam lazily at one end of the pool. At the other end Tom and Judy sat on the seats in the water talking with a young couple sitting next to them. Along with Bert, the man serving the drinks, they were the only people there.

Leaving the boys, Paige swam to where her parents sat. She was an excellent swimmer and was able to go half the length of the pool underwater. She came up for air and slipped under the water again. Surfacing next to her mother, she pushed her long wet hair out of her eyes then sipped a soda she had waiting there.

"Tired?" her mom asked.

"A little I guess." Actually, she was very tired. They all were.

"We'll get going," Judy said. "Go get the boys."

Paige slipped beneath the water once more and swam away, coming to the surface half way between her parents and her stepbrothers. She faced away from both, looking at a patch of shrubbery and flowers.

Wiping the water from her eyes she froze. Something in the shadows moved. Peering into the darkness she could see the shimmer of the pool reflected in a pair of dark eyes.

They stared at each other.

Feeling a chill run up her spine Paige took a few steps towards Tyler and Tommy, never looking away from the eyes that stared back at her.

As she moved the eyes followed her.

Feeling that chill run up her spine again she stopped and stared.

Suddenly, there was splashing. Paige let out a piercing scream.

3.

Something had her leg!

Pulling free Paige turned toward it. With a splash it came out of the water and lunged at her. There was a growl and a flash of something red.

It was Tyler.

When he started laughing Paige could see a pair of red rubber fangs in his mouth. He was forever wearing those fangs and trying to scare her.

Tom and Judy yelled at them from across the pool.

"Paige! Tyler! What are you doing? Stop it!"

"Oh man, you really got her," Tommy laughed.

Paige slapped at Tyler to chase him away then her attention returned to where she had seen the eyes.

"I think it's time to go," Tom announced.

Promising to behave, Tyler and Tommy pleaded for a little more time in the pool. While they did Paige swam along the edge of the pool peering into the darkness.

"No," Tom said, "You three go get ready for bed, we'll be right there."

Wrapped in towels Tyler, Paige and Tommy followed the lighted path to their cabana. Paige, wary of the shadows, hurried from light to light, trying to stay in the center of the path.

"Why did you have to scream like that?" Tyler asked.

"Did he scare you that much?" Tommy added.

"No."

"Then why did you scream?" Tyler prodded.

"I was scared," she said, "but not by you."

"Yeah right. I scared you."

They stopped near the cabana. Tyler held the key in his hand.

"You didn't scare me," Paige insisted. "There was something there, watching me."

"Where?" Tommy asked.

"In the bushes by the pool. I heard it. And I could see its eyes," she explained.

"What? Like an animal?"

"No," Paige said, thinking about it. "The eyes were bigger. Like your…like our eyes, but close to the ground, like crouching down."

Tommy laughed. "Maybe it was a goatsucker."

Paige ignored him. Hearing the parents coming she took the key from Tyler's hand and opened the door.

"They're already mad," she said, "Come on."

She was already in the room when Tom and Judy came into the courtyard.

Spotting the boys Tom said, "Come on you two, inside."

"We're just drying off," they said.

Knowing better than to push their luck Tyler and Tommy went inside without another word. Tom and Judy followed a few seconds later, closing the door behind them.

Late that night a *squall* blew across the island, announcing itself with thunder and lightning. Rain blew and dripped from the tile roofs. Along the paths the wind blew plants back and forth in front of the small lights that lit them sending wild shadows darting across the paths.

Moving quickly Tom came out of his cabana and scurried over to the children's. Fumbling with the key he opened the door. He stared in for a moment, trying to see in the dark. Finally, lightning lit the room.

Tyler and Tommy slept contently in one bed with the coconut between them. In the other Paige slept soundly, hugging a pillow to her chest.

With a smile Tom closed the door and hurried back to the comfort of his room.

"They're fine," he was telling Judy before he even closed the door. "You should see them," he said, going on to describe them to her.

After the door closed lightning flashed again. Something between the two cabanas—something that had looked like a shadow—moved forward for an instant before retreating back into the dark.

4.

By the time the children awoke the following morning the only traces of the night's storm were some leaves on the ground and a few damp spots in the sand. If they hadn't been told they would have never known it had rained. That is how late they slept.

When they went to breakfast most of the other guests were gone. By the time they finished the Olivers were the only people left on the deck. Sipping his coffee Tom looked at Tommy's coconut sitting among the dishes on the table.

"What's that thing doing here?"

"It's the pet I never had," Tommy answered.

Tom could only shake his head as they laughed. Just then the waitress, a tall black woman named Antoinette, came onto the deck carrying a pot of coffee. She wore her long hair tied atop her head with colorful ribbons, making her look even taller.

Spotting her Paige whispered to her mother. "Here she comes."

Stepping up to the table, Antoinette smiled broadly as she filled Tom's coffee cup.

"Antoinette," Judy said, "Excuse me."

"Yes mam," she said politely.

"I was wondering," Judy began, "if you could tell us where we could do some shopping."

"Well, there is a gift shop here, and several more in town."

"No, I mean good shopping," Judy explained, winking for emphasis.

"Oh, shopping," Antoinette said. She understood. "No, for some real shopping you must go to Belize City."

"All the way back there?"

"I am afraid so," Antoinette apologized. "But there are planes all the time."

"I know," said Judy. "Planes and boats and more boats and planes—I've made the trip once already, thank you."

"If you want to go I will be glad to help you with the arrangements," Antoinette offered. "Or I can go with you if you like."

"That's very kind," said Judy, "I'll let you know."

Once Antoinette had left Tommy was quick to speak up.

"I'm not going shopping," he sneered.

Paige told him he didn't have to go.

"No you don't," Tom explained. "That's the beauty of this trip. There is plenty to do and we can all do what we want."

"Snorkeling," Tommy called out, "And fishing with you."

"Yeah. And I want to go to those ruins you told us about," Tyler added.

Ever since they had begun planning this trip Tom had been telling the children about the pyramids and ancient ruins he wanted to visit. Now he was glad to hear Tyler wanted to go as well.

"Okay. We have time for all that," Tom assured them.

Feeling left out Paige spoke up.

"I want to do that stuff too," she said. "Maybe not fishing, but the snorkeling and stuff," she added, thinking about it.

"Okay," Tom said, "But how about today we just relax?"

He turned to Judy and teased her. "All this and you want to go shopping?"

That afternoon there were more people at the pool than had been there the night before. While the parents lounged in the sun, Tyler, Paige and Tommy swam. Still thinking of the night before Paige couldn't help but peek beyond the pool a few times.

Finally she swam to the ladder and climbed out of the pool near her parents.

"Where are you going?" they asked.

"To the bathroom."

Wrapping herself in a towel Paige left the pool area, headed toward their cabana. Half way along she stopped and looked around. Sure that no one was watching she left the path, cutting between two cabanas.

Peeking around a corner Paige saw what she was looking for. It was the girl she had seen on the beach. As she watched the girl crept along mysteriously, searching for something, or someone.

Paige followed her. She wanted to say hello but was afraid to speak up. Then the girl stopped and stood perfectly still.

Paige waited.

Suddenly the girl shouted, "Chupacabras!"

Stunned, Paige jumped.

Astonished, she watched as the boy from the boat came out from under a porch. Paige had had no idea he was there. Looking up he saw Paige. Realizing she had been followed the girl turned.

The three of them stared at each other.

When Paige returned to the pool, Tom and Judy were still lying in the sun with their eyes closed. She could see that her mother was dozing. Tom was too.

"Pssssttttt," she hissed trying to get the boy's attention.

"Tyler. Come here. Tommy," she whispered.

Finally they looked. Signaling them to say nothing, she motioned them to follow her.

"What?" Tyler asked in a loud annoyed whisper.

"Just come here," she answered impatiently.

The boys climbed out of the pool and followed Paige. Around the corner the girl and boy stood waiting.

Proudly, Paige introduced them.

"This is Natalie and Peto."

"Hi," said Natalie.

"Hello," Tommy replied.

Peto only nodded. Tyler did the same. The two of them stood and looked, each considering the other.

"It was Peto that I saw last night," Natalie said, hoping to break the ice.

"In the bushes?" Tyler asked.

"Si. We were playing," Peto explained. He spoke with an accent much like that of the man on the plane. "I didn't mean to scare your sister."

"That's okay," laughed Tyler, "It was pretty funny."

"Their parents work here," explained Paige.

She had told Natalie that it was her father, Bert, who was working at the pool the night before. He had been talking to their parents when all the screaming started.

"I saw you on the boat," Tyler said to Peto. Peto explained that his mother, Captain Mosa, was in charge of the resort's fishing boat and he often helped her. "My father is the carpenter," he added.

This reminded Natalie that she had something to tell Peto. "My Dad knows we were out last night," she said. Peto looked worried until Natalie said, "Don't worry, he won't tell."

She explained to Tyler and Paige that the two of them weren't supposed to be out after dark, Reaux, the manager said so. Still, they usually were.

Eager to do something with these new friends, Paige suggested that they come swimming.

Natalie shook her head. "We're not supposed to."

"What do you mean?" asked Paige.

Peto explained. "The pool is for guests."

Now Tommy, who had so far been quiet, spoke up.

"Then let's go to the beach."

"Yeah," agreed Paige, "We'll meet you there."

Tyler, Paige and Tommy went back to the pool to tell their parents where they were going. Natalie and Peto headed to the beach.

5.

The boys lingered in the shade where the beach met the tropical forest. Paige and Natalie stood near the water's edge, near the dock.

Listening to Peto, Tommy asked, "Where are you from?"

"Puerto Rico," Peto answered.

Tommy thought of Puerto Rico, the sunny green island in a shining sea he had seen from the air. Even the name—Puerto Rico—sounded exciting.

"How about you?" Peto asked.

"Pennsylvania," Tommy said, sounding bored.

"Pennsylvania," Peto repeated. To Peto it sounded like a far away place, one very different than his home. "Where is that?" he asked, then listened as Tyler explained.

"What were you doing last night?" Tyler asked.

"When I scared your sister?" Peto said. "We were playing a game."

"She's my step sister," said Tyler, before asking, "What kind of game?"

"Chupacabras."

"What?" Tommy blurted out.

Before Peto could repeat himself Tyler stopped him. "That's what the man on the plane called the goatsucker Tommy."

"Yes, El Chupacabras—the goatsucker," Peto agreed.

"We know what that is," Tommy said. "So," he asked, "how do you play?"

"Well," Peto began, "usually I am El Chupacabras and Natalie must find me before I find a victim."

"And Paige was going to be the victim?"

At that Peto just shrugs. Sometimes a game sounds strange unless you are playing it. This was one of those games.

"I know about goatsuckers," Tommy said. "He drew a picture of one," he added, pointing proudly to his brother.

"I _have_ pictures of them," Peto said, anxious to share his interest.

"Really," Tyler asked wide-eyed, "real pictures."

"Some. Some are drawings by people who have seen El Chupacabras. Come on."

Without a word to the girls the boys turned to go. Peto ran and Tyler and Tommy followed.

Down by the water Paige watched them go.

"Hey! Where are you going?" she called.

Tommy turned and tried to shrug while running, nearly falling down.

"To Peto's. It's right there," says Natalie, pointing right up the beach.

Sure enough Peto slowed and turned to a small house set back off the beach. Tyler and Tommy followed him onto the porch.

Natalie wasn't interested but when Paige began wandering that way she went along. She would rather play with Natalie herself; there were no other girls on the island to be her friend.

"That's a little house," said Paige, as they got closer.

Natalie had never really thought about it.

"I guess. Peto says it's way better than what they had in Puerto Rico. Our house is the same, but it's only me and my Dad."

No sooner had Peto returned to the boys on the porch when a voice called out from inside.

"Peto," called a man's voice, "Peto, is that you?"

"Si, Papa," he answered.

"Have you seen my glasses?"

"Your glasses?" Peto asked back, a bit confused. His father didn't wear glasses.

"Si. The red work glasses," his father explained, "The ones you were fooling with."

"No."

"Are you sure?"

"Si," Peto said, "I put them back in your toolbox. You were there."

When his father didn't say anything more Peto shrugged to his new friends and called their attention to the shoebox he had picked up off a small table. By the time the girls got there Peto had begun showing Tyler and Tommy the pictures he had cut out of magazines, books and newspapers.

Paige followed Natalie onto the porch.

"You and that stupid goatsucker," Natalie said to Peto. To Paige she said, "It's all he talks about. He says he is going to catch one. He is even digging a trap."

Peto gave her a *cross* look. He was serious about El Chupacabras. Ignoring her, he showed a picture to the boys. "I like this one."

"Cool," says Tommy. "It looks like yours Tyler."

It is a sketch of a goatsucker. Like Tyler's drawing it has fangs and claws and big red eyes. The caption under the picture was written in Spanish.

Tyler asked what it said.

"Ahh…" Peto started, working on *translating* the Spanish to English. "This Chupacabras was described as four feet tall, weighing about seventy pounds, with powerful *taloned* hind legs and thin clawed arms. It's face has a…" He struggles with the next word, then finished, "a lipless fanged mouth and huge red eyes."

"That's cool," said Tommy.

"El Chupacbras?" Peto asked.

"No," he said, "You can speak two languages."

Smiling Peto showed them more pictures, all drawings much like the first one. When he comes to one that looks like a photograph Tyler stops Peto.

"Is that a picture of one?"

"It is in a museum in Mexico."

"Where?"

"I do not know," Peto says. "When I catch mine I am going to put it in a cage like a zoo back in Puerto Rico."

Natalie laughed. "When you catch one he's going to suck your brains out. With a straw!"

Later, the five of them returned to the beach by the dock. As they did Natalie slowed.

"Peto," she said quietly. With a nod she directed his attention to where Reaux stood watching them.

"He doesn't like us," she explained to Tyler, Paige and Tommy.

"He doesn't like us around the guests, that is all," Peto explains, adding, "That is what my father says."

"Well, I don't like him," Natalie says, "He's creepy."

Ignoring Natalie, Peto told the boys, "Reaux has seen the chupacabras here on the island. That is why you will not see him out at night. He will not come out after dark."

As Peto is telling them this Tom and Judy join Reaux. Tom whistles for the children. While they wait for the children they chat with Reaux.

"You knew they were here?" he asks.

"Oh yes, they told us they would be here with their friends."

"The children's parents work here at the resort," Reaux told them, "If you do not want them associating with the children I will tell their parents."

Surprised at what he has said both Tom and Judy shook their head.

"No. No need for that," Tom said, looking at Judy.

That night the Olivers sat at the same table where they had eaten breakfast. Tyler *dubbed* it 'their' table. The chef himself, a smiling Jamaican man in a crisp white uniform, came out to take their order. They had met Chef—as he liked to be known—the previous evening. Tommy of course liked his accent, the same one he had heard at the airport; Paige admired his tall white hat. She had thought only cooks on television wore them.

"Did everyone have a good day," Chef asked.

"A great day," they all agreed.

"And you my friends," Chef said to the children, "Are you hungry?"

They certainly were and the told Chef so, loudly.

"Good," he replied, "I keep my job for one more day. Now, tonight, for the adults we have Larry baked. And for the children..."

"Larry?" interrupted Tommy.

"You remember," Paige said, "Larry the Lobster."

Chef liked to call the lobster Larry.

"I picked him off the reef myself, just this morning," Chef said.

"Really?" asked Judy.

"Yes mam. The reef is full of them," he explained, "The sweetest lobster this side of Jamaica mon. Now, for the children, I have Jerk Chicken."

Tyler, Paige and Tommy laughed. They had never heard of such a thing and thought the name was funny.

Chef turned to Paige. "And for you…" he teased, not finishing the sentence.

"Mashed potatoes," said Paige hopefully. The night before she had declared Chef's mashed potatoes to be the best anywhere and had eaten three helpings.

"A big bowl just for you," he said, "Better than last night."

"What's jerk chicken," Tyler asked.

"Jerk is a blend of seasonings from Jamaica, where I come from," Chef explained. "If you like spices, you like jerk mon."

Tyler nodded and Chef smiled. "One Jerk Chicken," he said before taking the other's orders.

Chef's 'Jerk' Chicken

Jerk Seasoning

4 Tablespoons Ground Allspice	1 Tablespoon Dried Thyme
1 Tablespoon Paprika	1 Teaspoon Ground Red Pepper
1 Teaspoon Garlic Powder	1 Teaspoon Onion Powder
1 Teaspoon Salt	½ Teaspoon Black Pepper

1 Crushed Scotch Bonnet Pepper (Optional)

Mix ingredients. 9Use 1—1 ½ Tablespoon per pound of meat.)

Jerk Chicken

2 Pounds Chicken Pieces   3 Tablespoon Chef's Jerk Seasoning

1 Tablespoon Soy Sauce

Toss Chicken, Jerk seasoning and Soy sauce in bowl until well blended. Allow to Marinate 1 to 2 Hours. Grill or Broil Chicken, turning frequently.

Before Chef could go to the kitchen and begin preparing their dinners Tommy and Paige stopped him. "She has a question for you," Tommy said, pointing to Paige, who blushed and giggled.

"How do chef's keep those hats up?" she asked, pointing to his tall white hat.

"Yeah, how do you?" the boys chimed in.

"Well, I cannot speak for all the chefs in the world mon," he said, "But for me…"

Like a magician revealing his secret he reached up and yanked his hat off. A tall ponytail of thick dreadlocks fell out.

"This is how I do it mon"

"Cool," said Tommy.

"Yeah. Really cool," Paige and Tyler agreed.

Later, after most of dinner had been eaten, Paige and Tommy worked at scraping the last of the potatoes from the bowl. Watching them, Tyler and his parents relaxed in the evening breeze. Tyler turned to his father.

"Dad," he asked, "did you ever hear of a goatsucker?"

"A what?" Judy asked.

"A goatsucker," said Paige.

Tom thought for a moment. "Well, when I was in Texas there was a bird there some people called a goatsucker, but I don't suppose that's what you mean."

It wasn't.

"No," said Tyler, disappointed. Dad could usually provide information on any subject.

"This is a creature that sucks the blood out of animals," Tommy anxiously explained, adding, "through their heads!"

Judy grimaced and said, "That's what I was afraid of."

Just then Tommy sucked hard on his straw in his near empty glass. There is a loud gurgle. He laughed. They all laughed.

Becoming serious again Tyler continued. "Peto says there is one on the island. He's going to catch it."

"He calls it 'El Chupacabras'," Paige added.

Not wanting the children to take such stories too seriously Judy explained that Peto might just be having fun with them. But both Tyler and Paige explained that they had heard of goatsuckers before meeting Peto.

"Tell him if he catches one I'll make him famous," Tom said, putting the subject to rest. "Now, let's get back to the cabanas, we're snorkeling early tomorrow."

Of course the children begged for "just a few more minutes" but Tom told them, "Not if you want to see Larry where he lives."

Leaving the restaurant, Tyler, Paige and Tommy ran ahead, while Tom and Judy strolled arm in arm. Done cooking for the night Chef sat near the kitchen door. They waved and wished him good night.

Thinking of the goatsucker Judy joked with Tom. "Maybe we should take Reaux up on his offer," she said, "especially with that Peto and his stories."

"What," Tom laughed. "That's just kid stuff. You should hear the stories I tell them," he teased, "it would make your toes curl."

Laughing together, they walked through the quiet tropical night. Behind them a boat passed, it's *wake* juggling the moon's reflection on the water.

"I wonder where they're going," said Tom.

6.

The next morning was brilliant, bright and clear. There was hardly a cloud in the broad blue sky and barely a ripple on the turquoise water.

Although it was early the Olivers were already out on the water, preparing to go snorkeling. They sat in a green fiberglass boat with low sides anchored out near the reef. They were listening to the instructions being given by Maura, a young lady from the resort. Felix, the young man in charge of the boat, had already handed them each a diving mask, snorkel and big floppy flippers. While they listened to Maura they tried on their equipment, laughing as their masks fogged up and joking when their flippers got tangled. Even Tommy, who was never awake this early was in a fine mood.

"This is one of the longest barrier reefs in the world," Maura explained, "so, along with all the fish you are going to see many kinds of coral. You'll see fan *coral*, that's the delicate, tall coral that grows like a fan, and brain coral, that's the big round ones. You'll know them when you see them."

"How about Larry?" Tommy interrupted.

"What's that?"

"*Langosta*," answered Felix in Spanish from where he sat back by the boat's engine. "Chef calls lobster 'Larry'."

"Oh yeah," she laughed, "plenty of them."

Maura continued explaining things to the Olivers.

"And again," she said, "the three things to remember are; number one, if you get water in your snorkel just surface and blow it out—it's no problem, number two, do not touch the coral—you can hurt it and it can hurt you—and number three, don't reach into any small spaces, there's nothing aggressive in the water here but you might startle something. Okay?"

Anxious to get in the water, everyone nodded in agreement. When they did their masks shook and their snorkel tubes wiggled above their heads.

"Let's go!" Maura said pulling on her mask. Sitting on the edge of the boat she rolled backward into the water. One by one the Olivers followed, each doing the same.

Paige was first, followed by Tyler and his father. Tommy and Judy were last, holding hands and squealing as they rolled back into the warm water. In minutes all were set and comfortably snorkeling along the water's surface. Even the floppy flippers felt fine in the water.

It was as if they were flying over another world. The sunlight shone through the water all the way to the seabed. It was bright enough that they could even watch their shadows cross the sea floor like the shadows of airplanes across a sunny soccer field.

The bottom was sandy and flat but covered with little ripples from the ocean's tide. To Tyler these ripples looked like sand dunes on a vast barren desert. But it wasn't barren. Here there was a shell, half buried in the sand, and over there some *kelp* waved like a tree in a breeze.

And now something moved!

It was a crab. It scurried sideways then stopped, waving one big claw before running off again.

Tyler smiled in his mask, thinking of all the times he had 'crab walked' in gym class.

Now he noticed the fish—fat lazy grouper in sandy camouflage, shining yellow-fin tuna swimming in a school and even a silver barracuda, with lots of small, sharp teeth. Intent on watching the fish Tyler was surprised when a person swam into view.

It was Maura. And right behind her was Paige.

Taking a deep breath through the snorkel Tyler dove and followed them down.

Once she saw that they were all comfortable diving Maura led them to the reef. This was completely different than the sandy sea bottom.

Corals, Coral Reef and Barrier Reef.

Corals are tiny sea animals with an *external* limestone skeleton. Corals join together and with these skeletons form coral or coral reef. Branches and layers are formed by the addition of new members. Older members of the colony die, leaving their skeletons behind for more corals to grow on.

Coral can grow into large and elaborate shapes often known by their appearance. Good examples of this are the fan coral, which looks like a lady's fan, or brain coral, which is large and round and looks like a brain.

Coral that continues to grow is known as a coral reef. Coral reef serve as a home to sea vegetation, such as algae, and a host of microscopic *marine* life. These many microhabitats and the productivity of the reef support a great diversity of sea life.

Small fish, sea urchins, sea cucumbers, brittle stars, and *mollusks* feed on the algae. Hiding in the caves and crevices of a reef are predatory animals such as crabs, wrasses (long, spiny-finned fishes), moray eels, and sharks. Coral reefs are also home to larger fish such as barracuda and grouper.

Coral reefs are of three types: fringing reef, barrier reef, and atoll.

Fringing reefs extend outward from the shore of an island or mainland, with no water between reef and land. Barrier reefs occur farther offshore, with a channel or lagoon between reef and shore. Atolls are coral islands, usually a narrow, horseshoe-shaped reef with a shallow lagoon.

If that had been a desert, as Tyler had imagined it to be, then the reef was the most incredible complex of mountains, caves, tunnels and towers imaginable.

Here the grouper hid in shadows barely moving and quick blue minnows flit about.

Maura pointed to a huge round ball that looked like rock but had thick rope like lines all over it. Then she pointed to her head.

Paige got it! Brain coral.

Tommy swam around to the other side of it. When he came back he had a small lobster in his hand. Teasing he held it out at Paige. Giving him an underwater scolding, his father waved his finger at him and motioned him to put it down. They all watched as it swam off, not forward, as they had expected, but backwards.

Soon Maura gathered them together on the surface.

"Follow me down," she announced, "and I'll give you each some food for the smaller fish."

Maura dove first. Taking some food from a pouch on her waist she demonstrated how readily the minnows came to it. Then she gave them each some food.

Instantly, clouds of little fish of all shapes and colors surrounded them. Some darted about alone, others moved in densely packed schools. Then, as quickly as they had appeared, they disappeared when the food was gone.

Coming to the surface Paige pulled the snorkel from her mouth. "Cool! That was like swimming in an aquarium."

Turning to Maura she asked, "Do you have more?"

Nodding yes Maura led Tommy and Paige back down to feed more fish. Tyler and Judy dove to the coral together, agreeing it was one of the most interesting things they had ever seen.

Studying a big fan coral Tyler looked to the bottom trying to see how it was attached. There in a dark *niche* he thought he saw something. He moved his body to let the sunlight shine in.

He did see something!

But he couldn't hold his breath another second. Kicking his flippers he swam to the surface. Judy was there treading water.

"It's beautiful, isn't it?" she said.

"Why can't you touch it?" Tyler asked as Maura surfaced with them. "Isn't it just like rock?"

"No, coral is alive," explained Judy. "Touching it can kill it."

"You can cut yourself too," said Maura, "Most of it is pretty sharp."

Back underwater Tyler returned to the hole in the coral. He peered into it. Whatever was in there was smooth and green. And it looked like there was something written on it.

The hole was just large enough to fit Tyler's hand. Carefully, nervously, he prepared himself to reach in. Then something touched his leg.

Twisting in the water he turned to see Maura there. He thought he was caught but instead she pointed to where a broad manta ray—bigger than him—had joined them. It looked like a huge underwater bat. And his family was swimming with it!

Maura led him to the surface.

"Here," she said, putting something in his hand. "Here is some food for that ray. Just don't step on its tail," she cautioned, "The *barbs* on the tail are the only part that can hurt you."

Tyler nodded but said nothing. He was a little bit afraid of such a large and strange looking creature. Then Tommy and Paige came to the surface.

"That was so cool," Paige exclaimed.

Looking at his brother Tommy said, "You have to try it."

"It feels like a little baby's mouth," Paige squealed. "If I can do it you can do it," she teased.

"Come on," Maura encouraged before pulling her mask back on.

Tommy and Paige followed her back to where the manta ray lingered. A moment later Tyler joined them. Nervously he approached the big flat fish and reached under to where its mouth was. He broke into a grin so big that air bubbles seeped from the corners of his mouth. It did feel like a toothless baby's mouth! It even tickled his hand!

7.

The cabana was cool and dark, a nice change from the bright sunlight outside Tommy thought. Lying on the bed he balanced his coconut on his chest and watched Tyler pace the room. His brother needed to relax.

Tyler stopped at the bathroom door. A hair dryer could be heard running behind it. It had been going for some time now. Tyler banged on the door.

"Come on Paige."

Finally the dryer stopped and Paige stepped out of the bathroom, her hair hanging in her face. Tommy laughed, calling her Cousin It. When she looked at him confused he said, "You know, Cousin It from the Addams Family."

"Whatever," she shrugged.

"What are you doing?" Tyler asked her.

"Nothing."

"Go and see what Dad and your mom are doing," he told her.

"You go," said Paige.

"See if they are going to eat," he said.

"Why can't you go?" Paige asked, wondering why Tyler was suddenly so impatient.

"We have to get changed yet," Tyler explained. "You were the one in the bathroom."

She looked at them. They were still in their bathing suits. And, she thought, she would never find out what was going on this way. Agreeing with Tyler she left, keeping an eye on him as she went.

As soon as the door closed behind her Tyler sat on the edge of the bed next to Tommy.

"Look at this," he said, digging in his bathing suit pocket.

He brought out the green stone he had seen in the coral. He had gone back to get it when everyone was busy with the manta ray. It was roughly round in shape and an inch or so across—about the size of a half dollar—and it was more or less flat.

"What is it?" Tommy asked.

"I don't know, but look."

Tyler turned the stone over. On the other side were scratches in it that made a picture. Above the picture there was a dot.

Tommy looked at Tyler. "It's a…"

"Yeah," Tyler interrupted, "It's a goatsucker."

Indeed, it could be a picture of a goatsucker.

While they studied the stone something moved by the window. Cautiously, a head appeared, looking in without being seen.

The next thing the boys knew the door flew open. There stood Paige. In his haste to hide the stone Tyler dropped it on the carpet.

"What's that?" Paige asked, a satisfied smile on her face.

Tommy, still holding the coconut, spoke up.

"It's a coconut. Don't you know anything?"

While Tommy laughed Tyler tried to hide the stone.

"Come on," she said.

"What?"

"That," she said, pointing to where Tyler's toes only partially covered the stone. Slowly she began moving toward the open door.

"I'll just tell Mom and Dad."

"Okay," Tyler relented, "just close the door."

"You can't tell anyone," Tyler said. "None of the adults especially."

Anxious to see what Tyler was hiding, Paige agreed. Looking at the stone she examined it thoroughly. The *etching* on it surprised her too.

"Where did you get it?"

"When we were snorkeling. I found it in the coral," Tyler explained. "That's why you can't tell anyone."

"Well, we have to tell Natalie and Peto," Paige said.

Just then the phone rang. It was an old phone and the loud, old-fashioned bell scared them stiff.

Then it rang again.

The three of them stared at the phone as if it had eyes and could see them. Tyler nudged Paige.

"Answer it."

She picked up the receiver as it rang again.

"Hello?"

"Oh, hi Mom," she said relaxing. "I am. And the boys are almost ready. Okay."

Paige hung up the phone and looked at the boys still in their bathing suits.

"Hurry up," she said, "They're going to eat."

Rather than wait for the children Tom and Judy went ahead to lunch, sitting at the usual table. Soon Tyler, Paige and Tommy came onto the deck passing Chef and Reaux sitting at a corner table with some papers in front of them.

Chef caught Tommy's eye.

"Hello little mon."

"Hello Larry," Tommy shot back.

Chef laughed and said hello to Tyler and Paige as well. All through lunch the children—especially Tyler—were distracted by every voice they heard, looking expectantly at every person that passed. Finally Natalie and Peto came onto the beach. Their father was the first to see them.

"Is that who you're looking for?"

"What?" asked Tyler, trying not to seem too eager.

"Your friends there."

"Yeah," said Paige, not at all worried about appearing eager.

"Can we go?" asked Tyler.

"Don't you want to come swimming," Judy asked Paige.

Paige was never one to pass on swimming.

"I want to tell Natalie about snorkeling," she replied.

"Me too," chimed Tommy.

"Okay," said Tom, "Just remember to come to the pool."

Before he had even finished speaking the three of them were out of their seats and headed across the deck.

"And remember to let us know if you are going anywhere," Judy called after them.

Before they ran out onto the beach Paige stopped Tyler and whispered in his ear, "Do you have the thing?"

Tyler felt at his pocket and nodded. It was there.

Reaux watched from the table in the corner.

"Those kids are up to something," he said to Chef who was busy writing. "What is that?"

"Those kids," Reaux said again.

Chef looked up to see the children running out onto the sand. "Those kids are busy being kids mon," he said, "Relax."

8.

A short way past Peto's house the children left the beach, taking a narrow path into the forest. Out of sight of the beach the path turned, turning back past Peto's house and going behind Journey's End. Tyler stopped the group there.

"Look what Tyler found," blurted Paige.

Tyler glared at Paige as he dug into his pocket. He had wanted to announce his find. As they gathered around he pulled the stone from his pocket. Though they crowded him he was sure to hand the stone to Peto first.

"Look," Tommy said, "Turn it over."

"It's pretty," Natalie said to Paige, "What is it?"

Paige shrugged. "I don't know," she said, "but it has a picture of a goatsucker on it."

"It does? Let me see."

Natalie made a quick grab for the stone but Peto turned away and continued studying it.

"Chupacabras," he whispered. "*Donde?*" he asked, "Where? Where did you find this?"

"In the water," said Tommy.

"*Aqui?*" Peto asked, "Here?"

Tyler answered. "No, where we were snorkeling. I found it in the coral."

Again Natalie grabbed for the stone. This time Peto let her take it.

"Down by the rocks at the end of the key?" asked Peto. "I saw you leaving this morning."

Tommy joined the girls in examining the stone. "It looks like coral, green coral," Natalie was saying.

"Let me see it," Tommy said. He still had not actually held the stone.

Looking at the picture on it he began rubbing the dot above the picture. Something about it felt funny. Rubbing just a bit harder he realized that it wasn't just a dot on the stone, it was a hole through the stone and the hole was packed with sand. He rubbed more. In seconds the sand fell away.

"Hey. Look at this," he announced.

"It's a hole in it," said Tyler amazed.

Looking, Natalie said, "It's a necklace."

Just then their surprise was interrupted by voices nearby. Not wanting to be seen on the path they quietly moved along.

Not far from where they had been Peto stopped the group again.

"Here is where I'm making my trap."

Natalie turned to Paige and said, loud enough for Peto to hear, "It's a hole."

Crouching, Peto pulled aside some palm branches revealing some rotting planks beneath. Moving these he uncovered a rough hole. It was deep, probably deep enough for Tommy to stand in without being seen.

"See," Natalie said, "It's just a hole."

"It's a big hole," Paige observed, impressed by the work that must have gone into it.

Past the trap the path split into two paths. While they were talking Tommy wandered over that way.

"Where does this go?" he asked.

"You don't want to go that way," Peto said, pointing to one of the paths.

Natalie explained. "That goes back to the *lagoons* behind the island. There are crocodiles back there."

"Really?" asked Tommy.

"Seriously?" asked Paige.

"What about that way?" Tommy asked, pointing to the other route.

"That goes down to the end of the island," said Peto, "Down where you were this morning."

Paige asked what was down there. Natalie only shrugged. Peto said, "Not much. Chef lives down that way."

Realizing that they had been gone some time Tyler said that they had better get back. Natalie returned the stone to Tyler while Peto hid his trap. She had been holding it all this time. Taking it from her Tyler saw she had put it on a string. He held it up, letting the stone dangle on the string. Obviously this was how it was meant to be.

"See," said Natalie proudly, "a necklace. Put it on," she coaxed, smiling at Tyler.

"Thanks," he said, but feeling shy he waited.

As they made their way back to the beach he slipped the string over his head when no one was watching. Looking down at it he decided he liked the way it looked against his t-shirt.

As they neared the beach they saw Reaux talking to Felix, the boy who had driven the snorkeling boat. By the time the children came off the path and onto the beach Reaux and Tyler had separated, their conversation done. Felix walked past them, saying something to Peto in Spanish as he did. He only laughed when Peto tried to answer him.

Though they didn't know what had been said the other children could see that it angered Peto.

"What did he say?" Tyler asked.

"Nothing," said Peto, "*Nada.*"

Quick to change the subject, he called out to Reaux, who was still nearby. When he waved Peto trotted to his side.

"What was that all about?" Paige asked Natalie as they slowly followed. She wanted to know what had made Peto mad.

"What?"

"Felix and Peto, what was that?"

"Felix." Natalie explained, "Before he came here, with Reaux, Peto got to run the boat most of the time."

"Really," said Tyler, "That's cool."

"But Reaux gave the job to Felix. He said Peto was too young."

"What did he say to Peto?" Tommy asked.

"Nothing," Natalie shrugged. "He just teases Peto about being young and stuff."

While they were talking Peto caught up with Reaux.

"Hello Peto. You haven't been down at Rattan, have you?" he asked, referring to the abandoned resort further down the beach.

"No," Peto was quick to answer.

"It's not safe. And not safe for the guests."

"I know," said Peto as the other children caught up with them. "Mr. Reaux, please tell my friends about El Chupacabras."

Reaux laughed. "Peto, let's not scare the guests away."

"No," Peto pleaded, "They already know. And I have told them you have seen El Chupacabras here."

Looking at them, Reaux let Peto talk him into telling his story.

"You have, have you? Then it can do no harm."

He began walking toward the dock, motioning for the children to join him. Tyler and Peto walk next to him, one on either side. Tommy, Paige and Natalie stay close, only a step away.

Reaux began his story.

"When I first came here I liked to walk at night, not late, but in the evening. Then, one night, I went out later than usual. It was a dark night; I remember there was no moon. I went to that path, the one you just came off of. I did not know then that it turns into two paths. Without knowing it I went on the path that leads to the lagoons."

"Are there really crocodiles back there?" Tommy interrupted.

"Oh yes, big saltwater crocodiles" Reaux cautioned, "Don't you go back there, especially at night."

Anxious to hear the story, Peto and Tyler objected to Tommy's interruption.

With a smile Reaux returned to his tale. "Well, as I walked down the path it seemed to me that someone was behind me. But of course when I turned to look there was no one there.

"Soon, I was near the lagoons. I could see the eyes of the crocodiles as they lie in the water waiting to catch something in their hungry jaws."

Reaux stopped walking. His eyes became large.

"Still I felt there was someone behind me but I had to stop. I stood very still. I don't know how long but I stood very still. Finally, when I was sure I heard some one behind me, I turned as fast as I could. But when I did I tripped and fell to the ground."

Picturing this the girls giggled. Reaux crouched to look them in the eye.

"No. It was good I did," he said. "When I looked up, there he was—Chupacabras. I had fallen just in time. He was looking for me."

Now Reaux acted the part of El Chupacabras, crouching and creeping from child to child. Letting his arms dangle at his side he curled his fingers up like claws.

"There he was, right above me. His claws hung right over my face. Looking up I could see his big red eyes, looking, looking..."

Coming to Tyler, Reaux's eyes lingered on the stone hanging against the boy's t-shirt. Awe struck by the story none of the children noticed.

"I am not ashamed to tell you I was so afraid I closed my eyes and lay there waiting for him to sink his fangs into me. Finally, he must have left. I did not hear him go, chupacabras move that quietly."

Reaux straightened up, signaling the end of his story.

"Since then I do not go out at night. I do all I have to do when it is light out. When it is dark I do not come out."

Beginning to walk away he said, "And I recommend you do the same my young friends."

The five of them stood silent as they watched Reaux walk away.

Later the children hung around the palm trees. The afternoon had become hot and lazy. Tyler lie across the tree that was sideways watching Natalie and Paige walk circles around the base of another palm tree. Tommy and Peto were watching the fishing boat come in. This meant Peto would have to go help his mother soon.

Finally Paige stopped circling.

"Come on," she said to her brothers, "we had better get to the pool."

"Yeah. Come on Tommy," said Tyler, although he didn't move yet.

Tommy turned to Peto.

"Tonight right?"

"Yes," answered Peto, "I'll bring a flashlight too."

"And the fish heads?"

"If they caught any fish today," Peto said.

Natalie looked to Peto and spoke up.

"I don't know about this," she said, sounding very worried.

"Come on, we've done it before," he said.

"Never with guests."

"Don't worry," Peto said, "We won't even go on the path."

Tyler swung down from his perch on the palm tree.

"Come on," he said to Tommy, "race you to the pool."

Off they ran and Peto started to the pier, leaving Natalie and Paige behind.

"See you tonight," Paige said.

"Yeah, tonight," was Natalie's answer, though she did not sound enthused.

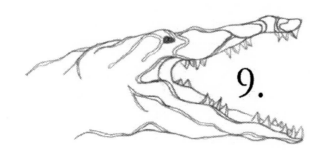

9.

As the sun set Tyler, Paige and Tommy waited near the palm trees for Peto and Natalie.

"This is going to be cool," said Tommy, "I hope he has the fish heads."

"Yuck," said Paige, trying not to think of them.

"Here they come," announced Tyler.

Peto and Natalie could be seen coming from the direction of Peto's house. Coming closer Natalie joined them. Peto headed toward the fishing boat and Tommy ran to catch up with him. By the time he did Peto had picked up a bag from near the boat.

"Do you have them?" Tommy asked.

Peto waved the bag in front of Tommy's face. "Nice and juicy," he said.

"Let me see them."

Joining the others under the palm trees, Peto handed Tommy the bag. As they walked off Tommy opened the bag and peered into it. Laughing, he said in a deep, dumb voice, "Fish heads."

Still laughing he ran to catch up with the rest of the children.

From the beach Peto led them through the *foliage*, carefully avoiding both paths and people. Finally, the brush cleared. Ahead of them was a path.

"This is the path down to the end of the island," Peto explained. Crossing it he plunged into the forest on the other side with Tommy hot on his heels. "Come on," he called back, "This way."

They found themselves only about ten yards from the lagoon. Tommy, Tyler, Paige and Natalie crouched behind a log. Peto left them, going toward the water. Darkness had fallen and it was hard to even see the water from where they were.

Peto rejoined the group behind the log.

"All set?" Tommy asked eagerly.

"All set," said Peto, "Now watch."

Pulling a small flashlight from his pocket he pointed it toward the water and turned it on. The beam of light poked out over the lagoon like a finger pointing into the sky.

Settling down, the light picked out the eerie image of mangrove roots reaching into the water. They looked like hundreds of fingers reaching down.

"What's that?" asked Paige, a chill running up her spine.

"A mangrove tree," Natalie began to explain. Not interested in trees, Tommy shushed them.

Now the light picked out something on shore near the water's edge. Peto whispered, "That's the fish heads."

"Fish heads," repeated Tommy in his funny voice.

Peto directed the light back to the water. Two eyes flashed when the light found them. They seemed to lie right on the water's surface.

"There's one," said Peto, holding the light steady on the eyes.

"What's with the eyes?" Tyler asked, wondering why they looked almost like reflectors on a bike.

"That's just from the flashlight," explained Peto.

He moved the light just a little and another pair of eyes appeared behind the first.

"There is another behind him," he said.

"No, there's two," said Tyler, spotting yet another pair of eyes lurking on the surface.

Peto clicked off the flashlight. It was now so dark they could barely see each other.

"Give them a minute," Peto whispered, "They'll be up for the fish heads."

"Fish heads," giggled Tommy again. He giggled until a small slap was heard. After a second of silence he giggled some more.

Anxiously, they waited in the dark. Finally, Natalie whispered, "Come on Peto."

He clicked the light back on. Sure enough there was a crocodile on shore pushing at the fish heads with its snout. It turned toward the light, hissing and showing its teeth.

There was another louder hiss—much closer!

A crocodile lifted its head from the other side of the log, turned and hissed again. It was so close Tommy could smell its hot breath!

Peto scrambled back from the log and the light went shining up into the trees. Tommy, who was next to him, jumped to his feet and froze. As the girls shrieked behind him, Tyler grabbed his brother, pulling him back.

Natalie turned and ran in the direction of the path they had crossed earlier. Paige turned to follow but fell as she did. Passing her on the ground, Tyler let go of Tommy and pulled Paige to her feet. They ran after Natalie with Peto and Tommy following.

The first one back on the path was Natalie. She took charge when Paige and Tyler came out of the forest behind her.

"Come on, this way," she said, leading them back in the direction of the resort. Though there was no longer any reason to, they ran.

Tommy was next out of the forest. Confused, he turned and ran the wrong way. Peto, coming out right behind him, shined the flashlight on his back.

"No," he called, "This way!"

Then Peto went silent. Tommy stopped right where he was. Shining past Tommy the flashlight picked out a pair of shining, dark red eyes looking at them from down the path.

Petrified, Tommy backed up, blocking the light.

The eyes disappeared.

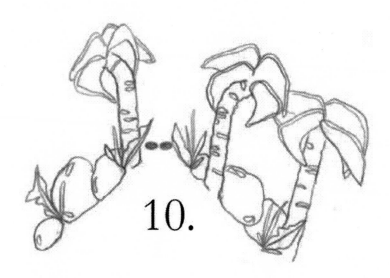

10.

Tyler, Paige and Natalie ran through the dark jungle toward the resort. Finally, they paused to catch their breath. Before they even had a chance to wonder where Tommy and Peto were the two of them came out of the dark, running toward them. They barely slowed down.

"Run," Tommy said breathlessly, "Come on!"

"We saw him. We saw him," was all Peto could say.

Tyler and Paige grabbed at the two of them to slow them down.

"Slow down," said Tyler.

"What are you talking about?" asked Paige.

"The goatsucker," exclaimed Tommy. "We saw the goatsucker!"

Peto tried to explain.

"Chupacabras was there. On the path, I saw him. We saw him," he stammered.

Already upset by their encounter with the crocodile, Natalie did not want to hear it. "Oh, shut up about that thing," she told them.

Still thoroughly frightened Tommy and Peto pulled away and began running to the resort. Unsure what to think about this Tyler and Paige followed, running as well. Natalie began to run, then slowed to a stubborn walk.

Bert, Natalie's father, was at the pool. The last of the guests had gone off to their rooms leaving him alone to clean up and turn out the lights.

Relaxing, he stood still for a moment listening.

The night was quiet but he thought he had heard something. He left the pool, returning a moment later with the small cart he used to put the pool supplies away. He hated using the cart, it was old and noisy, but it did the job.

Again he thought he heard something somewhere in the dark past the pool. But he couldn't be sure because the cart was making so much noise.

He stopped what he was doing to listen.

Without warning Peto and Tommy came running into the light at the opposite end of the pool, startling Bert. Paige and Tyler followed. Surprised to see Natalie's dad there they all came to a sudden stop.

"Hey Peto," Bert called to them, "where's Nat? You know the rules about being off the resort after dark."

Only now did they realize that Natalie was no longer with them. They tried not to panic.

Peto looked to the path behind them.

"She's coming," he called across the pool, "She's right behind us."

Bert began rolling the cart away. "Tell her it's time to get home, okay?"

He wasn't worried, the children knew their way around well, but he didn't want Reaux to see them out after dark with the guest's children. He would be sure to talk to Natalie about it.

There was an uncomfortable quiet while the children waited for Bert to leave. Finally, he rolled the cart out of sight.

"Where is she?" Peto asked the others in a loud insistent whisper.

"You don't think it got her, do you?" Tyler worried aloud. "Come on," he said to the others, ready to start back up the path in search of Natalie.

"No. It didn't get me," Natalie sneered as she stepped out of the dark.

"Natalie," they greeted her, glad to see she was safe.

"Are you okay?" Paige asked.

"Yes."

"Where were you?" Tommy asked.

Peto, who knew Natalie better than the others, could tell she was mad. He tried to change the subject.

"Natalie, your dad said…" he started to say.

"I heard him," Natalie cut him off and began walking.

"Where were you?" Tommy asked again as they followed her.

"I walked," was all she would say.

"What about the goatsucker?" Tommy asked.

Natalie turned to Tommy.

"Stop it," she said, "There was no goatsucker." Turning to Peto she continued, "There is no stupid goatsucker. It's a stupid game."

"No it's not," was all Peto would say. "El Chupacabras is here," he added quietly.

By now they were in the courtyard by the cabanas. Natalie stopped and looked to Tyler and Paige for support.

"I was with you," Tyler shrugged. He paused, looking at Peto and added, "But there's something here."

"No there is not," Natalie objected.

"What about this?" Tyler asked, pulling the mysterious medallion from under his shirt.

Still looking for support, Natalie looked to Paige.

"I don't know," Paige shrugged. She didn't want to hurt anyone's feelings.

Feeling alone Natalie turned and began walking away. Paige called after her.

Beginning to run, Natalie called over her shoulder, "I have to go." She sounded upset.

Paige was about to go after her when the door to her parent's cabana opened. Her mom stood in the door.

"Paige. Tyler and Tommy," she said sternly, "Where have you been?"

Peto lowered his head. "I better go," he said quietly, "*Manana.*"

"See you."

"Bye Peto."

"Your father is out looking for you," Judy said to the children. Silently, they walked to the cabana door.

11.

The next morning Tyler, Paige and Tommy were up and out early. Hungry, they went to eat by themselves, waiting at their table for their parents. *Humbled* by their experience the night before and mindful of their parent's warnings they sat quite quietly. Antoinette greeted them then went directly to the kitchen door, announcing their arrival to someone inside.

Chef peeked out.

A moment later he crossed the deck to their table, his smile a little less broad than usual.

"Good morning children," he said, "Are you tired after your adventure last night?"

Chef watched as the three young faces staring up at him changed expression from smiling, to confused, to guilty.

"Ah, that's right," Chef continued. "Chef heard you screaming and sneaking out on the paths last night. Not to worry though, I will not tell anyone. It is not my business. But, be warned, that is no place to be wandering at night. It is not safe."

He gave them each a hard stare then turned to go. But before he could Tommy spoke up.

"Don't you live there?" he asked.

"There is a difference between living there and looking for trouble there," he said.

Finally Chef left, but before they could discuss what he had said their father rushed to the table. Leaning in close he spoke quietly, but urgently.

"Don't laugh," he said, "That's all I'm saying. Don't laugh."

He sat and waited.

Judy came onto the deck wearing some sort of mismatched safari outfit she had assembled from Tom and the children's clothes. She wanted to be ready for today's trip into the jungle to the pyramids of Altun Ha.

She had on a pair of Tom's shorts—which were just a little too big—and one of Paige's shirts—which was much too small. She had borrowed Tyler's hiking boots, which she wore with a pair of rolled down white socks. The outfit was finished with a bandana of Tommy's tied around her neck and Tyler's baseball cap atop her head.

Trying not to laugh the children buried their faces in their menus. Fortunately, Antoinette came to the table.

"Good morning," she said cheerfully.

"Good morning," answered Judy.

Taking in Judy's outfit, Antoinette asked, "Are you going somewhere today mam?"

Hearing this the children exploded in laughter.

Out on the open water the boat from ran full speed across the waves. Felix sat in the back next to the boat's powerful outboard motor, one hand on the throttle.

Maura rode in the front of the boat. Paige sat next to her. Tyler and Tommy sat behind them, then Tom and Judy. Though she tried to look relaxed, Judy was tense, gripping her seat tighter each time the boat slapped a wave.

After traveling like this for quite some time the boat slowed enough that it stopped slapping the water. Felix turned the boat's engine, steering the boat toward a calm, open *estuary*. Judy relaxed as Maura spoke.

"This is the mouth of the river," she explained. "We will travel up it several miles to a small village where we will meet our vehicle."

Where the river met the sea the water was shallow and there were many *channels*. Felix turned the boat this way and that, finally finding the narrow, deep path that was the river. Soon the boat was again speeding along, the mangrove trees that hung over the river making the passage seem narrower than it really was. A mile or so along Maura signaled Felix, who slowed the boat, letting it float to a stop.

They peered into the tropical forest that shrouded the river. There wasn't much to see, the forest was thick and dark. Now Paige could see the mangrove roots she had only glimpsed in the dark the night before. They did indeed look like fingers, or hands, reaching into the water. Under these roots it was dark, mossy and moist.

Maura spoke up.

"As we go up the river it is not likely that you will see much wildlife, maybe a croc or two. Most of it is *nocturnal*," she explained. "That means it is only active at night. But there is something you will see plenty of. All around you in fact."

Maura pointed to some trees close to Judy's side of the boat.

"Do you see those dark, kind of shiny leaves there?" she asked, "The ones just hanging."

"Where?" Tommy asked.

Judy helped by leaning toward the leaves and pointing to them, her painted fingernails almost touching them.

"Yes, those there," Maura said. "Well, they're not leaves. They are bats."

Judy shrieked and pulled her hand back. The boys laughed as Tom consoled his wife, trying to hide his smile. In the front of the boat Paige huddled next to Maura. In the back of the boat Felix laughed, perhaps a bit too long.

"Don't be frightened," Maura said, "They are sleeping. We couldn't wake them if we tried," she assured Paige.

Tyler turned to Felix.

"Vampire bats?" he asked.

Felix shrugged. Maybe he hadn't understood him thought Tyler.

"Cool," Tommy said as the boat started up the river again.

After another mile the boat rounded a bend and slowed. Ahead was a clearing on the riverbank and beyond it several shacks. Felix steered the boat to shore, running it up on the bank and *grounding* it. Maura jumped out of the boat and pulled it further on to shore.

Two children and a dog watched them from a distance. They stood near what looked like the beginning of a road.

Anxious to get out of the boat, the children followed Maura. Trying to climb out Tommy slipped, but didn't fall out of the boat.

Felix laughed.

"Careful," he said, "You don't want the crocs to get you."

Felix laughed some more and all three children wondered if he too knew about their close call the night before.

By the time they were all ashore a big old van was coming out of the jungle. The dog barked as it followed the van to the riverside.

The van was old, but clean, with plenty of room. A tall man in a plain tan uniform was their driver. His name was Simon Paul and he would also be their guide at the pyramids. He was both friendly and eager to take the Olivers there. As they loaded the van Simon Paul explained that he had been one of the many men who had helped *archeologists* unearth the lost city they would see. Even Tommy could tell that he was quite proud of this.

Once they were in the van the children knelt on their seats and watched the dog chase the van up the road. They laughed until the van hit a jarring *rut* in the road. Flying out of their seats they nearly bounced their heads off the ceiling.

Seeing them bouncing in his mirror Simon Paul said, "You may want to keep your seat belts on."

12.

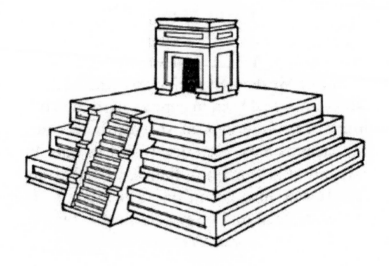

"Here we are," said Simon Paul, bringing the van to a stop.

Eagerly, Tom climbed out as Judy and the children looked around from inside the van.

It didn't look like any *tourist* attraction they could recall. There were no buildings, no people, not even a parking lot. There was just jungle. A little unsure of this place they slowly climbed out of the van and gathered around Tom, who seemed quite excited.

"Where is everything?" Tyler asked.

"Yeah," Paige agreed, "What's this?"

Tom *discreetly* signaled them to be patient as Simon Paul approached.

"Where's the city?" Tommy asked.

Simon Paul waved his arms in a gesture that *encompassed* the jungle all around them. "The city of Altun Ha is all around you," he said. "I will teach you how to see it. Come along," he added, starting up a path.

He stopped where the path bordered a large stone depression in the ground. Shaped like a bowl, it was broad and smooth—smooth enough to skateboard in thought Tyler. Simon Paul turned and pointed.

"See here this stone bowl and that dry creek bed. In the time of the Maya they lined this with clay and there, at that, a dam was built, making this a *reservoir*. This was the first step in the building of the city of Altun Ha."

Further along Simon Paul stopped again, this time to show them where stone had been cut from the same dry creek bed. The stone, he explained, was used to build with and the hole left in the creek bed became another reservoir as the city grew.

"You take water for granted," he told the children, "but for ancient people having a constant supply of clean water was a great achievement."

The Mayan Mystery

The Maya were an ancient Native American people who lived in what is now Central America. They were an advanced people who built huge stone pyramids and cities. They recorded their history in hieroglyphics, a picture language. The Maya were also accomplished mathematicians and astronomers.

The Maya reached their peak between the years 300 and 900 AD. During this time they built great cities, many of which grew to tens of thousands of people. The Maya then left their cities and returned to living in the jungles. Still, they dominated the region until the Spanish came in the 16th century.

Most of the Maya were farmers. Their crops included maize (corn), beans, squash, avocados, pineapples, papayas, and cacao. Cacoa was made into a chocolate drink. They ground corn on stones and mixed this with water to cook as tortillas. Rabbits, deer, and turkeys were hunted. Fishing also supplied part of their diet.

Mayan writing used pictures to represent either entire words or sounds, which could be combined to form words. These pictures, or glyphs, were carved into stone or painted onto walls for all to read. They often told the history of a city or the deeds of its heroes.

Recent advances in reading Mayan are bringing a better understanding of the Maya and their way of life. Even though, why the Maya abandoned their cities and returned to the jungle remains a mystery.

Eventually this same path came to a steep hill. Leading them up it Simon Paul turned to Tyler.

"What do you see here?" he asked, "What can you tell me about this hill we are on?"

Tyler looked around then noticed something.

"These rocks here, and those up there don't look like they belong here. They look like the rocks from that *quarry* thing you showed us."

"Very good," Simon Paul said. "Perhaps some day you will be an archeologist. So, what can you tell us about this hill?"

"Somebody built it?" Tyler guessed.

"Si," said Simon Paul, "This hill is made of layers of material from all over this site. This is actually the side of the city's central *plaza*." Coming to the top of the hill he hurried them along, "Come. See."

As they got to the top of the hill two pyramids—each at least a hundred feet tall—came into view. Along with them were several smaller stone buildings.

They were speechless. Tom smiled when Judy finally said "wow".

"Si," Simon Paul agreed. "Wow. It is very dramatic. And that is no accident; it was all carefully planned centuries ago. If you had been alive then you would have come up stairs to this very spot. Some of those stones you stepped on coming up here were once part of just such a staircase. And all this *plateau* was paved with stones such as these and made smooth with white plaster."

With that he led them to a spot where some of the original stone paving had been restored. It was nearly as smooth as the patio outside their back door at home.

The climb to the top of the pyramid left them breathless but taking in the view they agreed it was worth the effort. The ruins of Altun Ha were spread out before them and beyond that was only jungle, a green carpet as far as the eye could see.

Simon Paul crouched down between the children, pointing to direct their gaze.

"Do you see there and there, those mounds, those green mounds?"

"There's another one," said Tommy, pointing off in another direction.

"Si," Simon Paul agreed, "Those are other, smaller pyramids that have not even been uncovered. They are also part of the city. It once covered more than five square miles."

"How many people lived here," Tommy asked.

"Ten, maybe twenty thousand."

Paige turned to Tom. "How many live in our city?"

Tom thought. "Well," he said, "Not many more than that. Maybe twenty five thousand."

When they came back down in front of the pyramid, Tom had the children pose in front of the huge figures carved into the stone blocks there. As they did Simon Paul explained that these figures, with their exaggerated features, represented the Sun and Moon Gods that were part of the Mayan religion.

Next, Tom and Judy posed with the children while Simon Paul took the picture. Finally, Tom and Judy posed together, without the children. Tyler took this opportunity to ask if they could look around by themselves. Thinking of the night before, the parents were hesitant.

"Okay?" Tyler asked impatiently.

"Alright," said Tom. He and Judy watched as they ran off to explore some of the smaller buildings.

These smaller ruins were fun to explore. The blocks of stone that had once been the walls of buildings now stood without roofs. Moving through them was like moving through an ancient maze.

In some places the stones had been toppled and they could climb over them. At one such spot Tyler climbed over a block and found himself alone. He was behind a wall and close to the jungle. Deciding to hide from the others he ducked down close to the mossy wall. He wasn't there long before he called out to Tommy and Paige.

"Hey," he said, "Come here. Look at this."

Climbing over the stone blocks Tommy and Paige found Tyler standing in front of a weathered and mossy stone panel.

"Look."

Paige looked but didn't see anything.

"Look," Tyler repeated, "On this stone."

Tommy shrugged. He didn't see anything either.

"Look at the drawing on it," he said, using his finger to trace something carved into the rock.

"So?" said Paige.

"It's a chupacabras."

Paige shook her head. "No it's not."

"Yes it is," Tyler insisted, "Look."

The moss that had grown over it obscured whatever had been carved into the stone. Eager to prove his point Tyler pulled the medallion from under his shirt and compared it to the lines he had traced.

"It's the same thing," he insisted.

"So what," said Paige, "Get over this goatsucker stuff." Remembering the warning they had got the night before she added, "You're going to get us all in trouble."

Then she sat down and watched Tommy and Tyler study the panel. They hadn't been at it long when their parents called them.

It was time to eat.

They ate lunch at a picnic table under a *thatched* roof that provided shade from the noonday sun. While they enjoyed the grilled chicken and red beans with rice that Simon Paul had brought with him (there was no snack bar or restaurant) the children questioned him about Altun Ha and the people that had lived there.

"Have you ever found anything here?" Tommy asked.

"Many things have been found here," said Simon Paul.

Excited by the possibilities he imagined Tyler asked, "Relics? Or treasure? Buried stuff?"

"The most important thing found at Altun Ha is Kinich Ahau, the giant *jade* head," he explained. Simon Paul was very proud of the ancient city and the part he had played in its exploration. It showed when he spoke of it. "It is the largest such figure found in all the Mayan world. It is round, and about the size of a softball and weighs nearly ten pounds."

"Where was it," Paige wanted to know, "In the pyramid?"

"Not in the pyramid, under the pyramid," Simon Paul said. He explained that the Maya built their temples on top of one another. "They considered the spot, the location of the temple to be as important as the building itself. The largest pyramid here—the one we climbed—is actually built on top of two older temples. Kinich Ahau, the giant jade head, was found in the oldest."

"What's jade?" Tommy asked.

"Jade is a green stone, sacred to the Maya."

"Green like…" Tommy thought for a moment then asked, your ring?"

Tyler and Paige breathed a sigh of relief. Both had feared that Tommy was going to say something about the medallion Tyler wore.

Simon Paul looked at his ring then held it out for all three to see. "Yes, this is jade," he said, "but it is a very small piece."

Looking at that ring Tyler knew immediately that the stone medallion he had found was also jade. It looked so much alike.

"Where did the jade for the giant head come from?" he asked.

"No one is certain if it was mined nearby or found elsewhere," shrugged Simon Paul. "Altun Ha traded with many other Maya cities so who knows, it may have come from the mountains or even from the sea."

Paige had been watching Simon Paul closely. Noting the pride with which he spoke she finally asked, "Are you a Mayan?" She could imagine him having lived here quite happily all those years ago.

"Am I Maya?"

Again Simon Paul shrugged. "It is hard to say. When the Maya left their cities they vanished back into the forest. I am mostly Indian—my family has lived in these forests for many, many, many years. So, it is likely that I am descended from the Maya. I like to think so."

"I think you are," said Paige, which seemed to please Simon Paul greatly.

"Why did the Maya leave the cities?" asked Tyler.

"That we don't know," Simon Paul said. Smiling, he added, "Perhaps you will be the one to answer that question."

Now Tyler smiled. This place, with its ancient stones and *intricate* history, and the way Simon Paul spoke of it, made that seem possible. "Could you show us more?" he asked.

13.

That night a full moon shone through the window of the children's cabana, dimly lighting the room. Tyler and Tommy slept together with the coconut between them. Paige slept peacefully in her own bed.

They had returned from Altun Ha late and tired. After diner, which the Olivers ate alone on the deck, and a quick swim, they had been eager to get to bed. The children didn't even mind not seeing Peto or Natalie that day.

The three of them were sound asleep when a shadow passed through the room. Something moved past the window.

A breeze passed through the room as the door opened and closed.

Illuminated only by the pale moonlight a dark crouching figure leaned over Paige and stood very still for a moment. It turned and stood over the boys' bed.

The sound of its raspy breath could be heard over the peaceful whispers of the children's breathing.

Moving slowly but surely a thin arm reached out, carefully pulling the sheet away from Tyler's neck. Pulling it further it bared his chest as well. There the smooth jade medallion glimmered in the moonlight.

The other hand reached out to Tyler.

When it came to his chest the hand turned over revealing a single, hooked, blade-like claw. The claw slipped under the cord with the medallion on it, cutting it with ease.

Stepping back from the bed, the figure stood upright for a moment. Just then, Paige turned in her bed, opening her eyes for a heartbeat before closing them.

For an instant, all was still.

Then she screamed.

Startled, it crouched and looked at her. She stared into the red, elongated eyes of a chupacabras.

She screamed again.

Across the small room, the boys awoke, Tyler lying still and confused, Tommy bolting upright.

Now the goatsucker hissed menacingly, turning back and forth from one bed to the other as it backed toward the door. All three children were frozen with fear until Tommy grabbed the coconut and hurled it at the intruder.

The goatsucker yelled, hissing as it fled.

"I hit it," Tommy yelled, "I hit it!"

"But I hit it," Tommy insisted.

The lights were on and their parents were in the room with them. Hearing Paige's screams and Tommy's yelling Tom and Judy had come quickly. Once they had calmed the children and investigated, finding no sign of anyone or anything having been in the room, they had set about reasoning with them.

"No you didn't buddy," said Tom, "you thought you hit something."

Judy sat with Paige, comforting her.

"It was that thing," said Paige, "that goatsucker."

"There's no such thing," said Judy, looking into her daughter's eyes. "You had a nightmare honey. You woke up screaming and scared. And that scared the boys."

Tom sat between the boys on their bed. Patting Tommy's leg he said, "You probably threw it at a shadow."

Raising his voice a bit, Tom spoke to all three children. "Now, once and for all, there is no such thing as a goatsucker or chupacabras. It is a myth, a legend, okay? I don't want to hear anything more on the subject."

Judy agreed.

"No more goatsuckers, okay?"

While they were talking Tyler felt at his neck. Finding the cord hanging there without the medallion he realized why the goatsucker had come. He looked to Tommy and Paige but said nothing. They didn't notice.

Having said all he was going to, Tom got up go. As he did Judy said, "I'm going to stay here with Paige."

"Alright, I'll see you in the morning."

He watched as they settled back into bed, Judy with Paige, Tyler and Tommy together. On his way out the door his toe touched the coconut.

Picking it up he handed it to Tommy. Winking, he said, "Here, just throw it at Judy if she starts snoring. That's what I do."

Pulling the door closed behind him Tom was startled by Reaux, who was standing in the courtyard.

"Hello."

"I was told there was a disturbance," asked Reaux, "An intruder?"

"No," said Tom. "No, I don't think so."

"But I was summoned."

"No, I think it was a nightmare," Tom explained, "A bad dream, you know?"

"Oh, I see," said Reaux. "The children, are they alright?"

"Yes."

"Everyone is alright?"

"Yes," Tom assured him, explaining, "You get used to these things as a parent."

"Good then," said Reaux. "I will be going. I don't like the night."

Tom returned to his room as Reaux walked away. Hearing Tom close his door Reaux paused, looking around the courtyard suspiciously before leaving.

Back in the children's cabana all was quiet. Judy held Paige, who was still shaking with fear. Tyler slid close to Tommy in their bed. He whispered to his brother who turned to face him.

"The stone is gone," Tyler whispered, "It took it."

Hearing their whispers Judy said, "Quiet over there."

14.

The following morning brought another beautiful day, perfect for what was planned. This was the one day the boys and girls would split up. Tom and the boys would go fishing while Judy, Paige and Antoinette were off shopping.

Even though everybody was getting along well, all were looking forward to the time apart. Paige was anxious to go shopping with her mother, something they always enjoyed together, and the boys always anticipated doing something extra ordinary with their father, and deep-sea fishing would certainly be just that.

They all met at the dock. Tyler and Tommy waited on shore while Tom walked the girls out to the waiting water taxi. He kissed Judy goodbye and helped Paige into the boat. As she climbed into the boat with them Antoinette grinned and teased, "Don't you worry Mr. Oliver, I will only let them spend half of your money."

"Thank you," he smiled, "I appreciate that. See you tonight," he called as the boat pulled away.

He walked back to shore where the boys waited. Together the three of them headed to the fishing boat. They could see Peto's mother, Captain Mosa, on deck. When Peto came up from below, Tyler and Tommy both pointed.

"Hey, there's Peto," they exclaimed and ran ahead.

Soon Captain Mosa was at the controls on the boat's *bridge*. This was atop the cabin, high above everyone else. Peto stood ready to cast off. When the order came he loosened the ropes tying the boat and threw them ashore.

Out past the barrier reef the boat cruised at a good speed. Tom, Tyler and Tommy watched as Peto rigged the fishing lines they would use that day.

To some he attached *elaborate* lures with long colorful streamers that would trail in the water behind them. On other lines he put silver baitfish on long heavy hooks, tying the bait to them with thin wire.

Knowing his friends were watching Peto worked quietly and efficiently, doing his job as his mother expected him to. Tyler and Tommy watched with interest but were sure not to interfere, knowing he had a job to do.

Only when he was done did Tommy ask Peto, "Where do you go to the bathroom?"

Peto put the last fishing pole in its holder then led his friends below *deck*. As soon as they were there Tyler stopped Peto.

"Peto, it was in our room last night! It stole the necklace."

"What?" Peto asked, unsure what they were talking about.

"Last night," said Tommy.

"Chupacabras," said Tyler, "A goatsucker. It was in our room. It stole the stone from me."

"And I hit it with a coconut," Tommy added.

"What?" Peto could not believe what he was hearing! "Did you see it?"

The boat's engine growled steadily as the boys launched into an excited discussion of the previous night's events.

Left alone on deck Tom climbed the narrow ladder to the boat's bridge.

"May I?" he said, asking the captain's permission before joining her on the bridge.

"Si. Please do," said Peto's mother, stepping aside to make room for Tom.

Standing beside Captain Mosa, Tom admired the boat and the way it seemed to flow through the water. Seen from the bridge the ocean was an inviting blue expanse, speckled with white caps.

"Nice," he said, "Very nice."

"Is a beautiful boat," Captain Mosa agreed. "Better still," she laughed, "they pay me to run her."

"I envy you," said Tom sincerely.

Standing there at that moment Tom thought that this must be a nice way to live, one that he would enjoy himself. He thought about this while Captain Mosa listened to voices on the boat's two-way radio. When the chatter stopped Tom spoke up.

"So," he said, "tell me about El Chupacabras."

"That boy," said Peto's mother, shaking her head and sighing. It was an expression parents everywhere knew.

"El Chupacabras—the goatsucker—is one of those stories that won't go away, like your Big Foot stories. The stories first began when I was a young girl back in Puerto Rico, around 1980 or so. Everyone was talking about it even though there was no proof these things existed. You believed if you wanted to believe. Now the stories have spread but most people take them for what they are—just stories."

She stopped and smiled, raising a finger. "Except for Peto, he knows better."

Tom agreed, "They always know better."

"Yes, but where we come from," Captain Mosa said, "there is a village nearby whose mayor—Mayor Soto—has built his career on promises to rid the village of chupacabras." She shook her head and frowned. "Tales of expeditions and stories. This Soto, he has made himself a hero to many—including Peto. It makes it hard to explain when even adults behave as if the stories are true."

That said Captain Mosa turned her attention to the boat's controls. Pulling two chrome levers back toward herself she slowed the boats engines.

"They'll grow out of it," Tom said.

"I hope so, "Captain Mosa said, "If he ever does catch one what am I to do with it?"

Below deck Peto heard the boat's engines slow. He was already on his way up when his mother called to him.

Judy was relieved to arrive in Belize City. Finally, after the ride in the water taxi, another ride in the small plane, and a ride in a cramped auto taxi they arrived in the shopping district, ready to go.

Paige tried to take it all in. It was like a scene from a movie. People and carts crowded the streets, slowing any cars that tried to pass to a crawl. The people moved from shop to cart and back again, calling to each other and *haggling* with the merchants. Though it seemed a fun jumble, moving through the crowds made Paige uneasy. She didn't like being that close to strangers.

Antoinette explained that today was the traditional market day. This meant that many people from towns and villages outside the city had come in to buy and sell. Since they only traveled to the city once every few weeks or more it was an important day to them, it was an event.

Paige paused and listened to a customer and a merchant bargain. They went back and forth trying to arrive at a price that was good for both of them. It wasn't like at home where the price was marked and that's what you paid!

"Stay close honey," said Judy, urging her along.

Paige tried to hear what the final price was but the two were still haggling.

"Around the corner are the jewelry shops," said Antoinette, eager to lead the way.

Turning the corner both Paige and her mother were relieved. This street was also crowded, but not nearly as much. Here at least there was room to move.

And move they did—from stand to cart to store, trying on jewelry and comparing their choices. In time Paige came to a small stand in front of a dark and uninteresting looking store. On the stand was jewelry, some of which looked much like the medallion Tyler had found. The sign above it said the jewelry was 'native'.

Intrigued by what she saw, Paige stopped and began looking through the selection. The shopkeeper watched her through the dusty window.

"Do you like?" asked Antoinette.

"Yeah," said Paige, "They're neat."

"It is native jewelry, made by the Indians," Antoinette explained.

"What's it made of?" asked Paige.

"Most is soapstone, it is easy to carve," Antoinette said, looking quickly through the selection, "but some is coral or shell."

"Any jade?" asked Paige.

Antoinette looked up at the shopkeeper still watching from the window. "No, I doubt that," she answered, "Not here."

While they had been looking at this Judy had walked on ahead. Now Paige and Antoinette moved along to catch up with her, leaving the jewelry stand behind. As they left the shopkeeper came out. He stood and watched them go.

"Are they Maya?" Paige asked as they walked.

Antoinette looked her way. "Mayan? Who?"

"The Indians who made the jewelry."

"I don't know," Antoinette answered. "They may be descendants of the Maya. Why?"

"Some of it looks like Maya jewelry," Paige answered, "That's all."

Antoinette looked curiously at the girl, wondering where she would have seen Mayan jewelry. Then she laughed, "If it were Mayan it would be worth much. It would belong in a museum."

By now Judy had wandered across the street. Seeing Paige and Antoinette looking for her she waved and called out, "Come on, I've struck gold!"

She stood in front of a store specializing in gold jewelry, her favorite. Crossing the street Antoinette and Paige followed her in.

Though she was at first dazzled by all the gold—rows and rows of gold chains, bracelets piled high on wooden posts and earrings strung on long *taut* strings— Paige soon became bored watching Antoinette and her mother sort their way through it all. She went to the window to watch the people on the street.

To her surprise Reaux walked past, right outside the store. Although she really couldn't say why, she stepped back from the window, not wanting him to see her.

She watched as he hurried directly to the stand she had just left. Reaux approached the shopkeeper still standing next to the native jewelry stand. They talked for a moment and then Reaux pulled a pouch from his pocket. From the pouch he pulled something, something green. Now the shopkeeper, who had looked bored and rather annoyed with Reaux, became interested. Putting his hand on Reaux's shoulder and smiling, he led him into the shop.

Paige stared at the shop, waiting for Reaux to come out. She looked away only to check on Antoinette and her mother. For what seemed like an eternity they looked at jewelry as Paige wished they would hurry. She wanted to get across the street before Reaux left that shop.

She even flirted with the idea of slipping out of the shop and going over there by herself but she couldn't, it would worry her mother too much if she were to disappear.

Finally, Judy and Antoinette were ready to leave. And Paige hadn't seen Reaux come out of the shop across the street.

Leaving the gold jewelry store Paige asked, "Mom, can I get some native jewelry?"

"What's that honey?" Judy asked.

"It's right over there," said Paige, pointing. "Come on."

Before her mom could say a word Paige was off. A car beeped its horn. She had stepped into the street without looking and had nearly been hit. The car stopped and she ran to the other side.

Judy and Antoinette followed, catching up with Paige at the stand in front of the shop. Paige pretended to be looking at the jewelry on the stand while she looked into the store. She couldn't see in very well.

Her mother looked at the jewelry on the stand and shrugged.

"Maybe there's more inside," said Paige. Again, without waiting for an answer she led the way.

Inside the shopkeeper looked up from a table behind the counter. He watched warily as Paige made a quick circuit of the store. There was no jewelry inside, just odd assorted items, some of which looked old. More importantly, there was no sign of Reaux.

"May I help you?" asked the shopkeeper, standing to look at the girl.

Startled, Paige stared at him. Judy and Antoinette came through the door and finally, Paige spoke up, "Is there any jewelry in here?"

"No. All the jewelry is outside."

"Oh. Thank you," Paige said to him. Turning to her mother she repeated his words. "All the jewelry is outside."

Passing Judy and Antoinette she went back outside. Puzzled, the two women looked at each other wondering what had gotten into Paige.

Outside, Paige eventually chose two identical necklaces and bought them with her own money.

15.

It was late afternoon when Paige and the women returned to the resort. Antoinette was first out of the boat. She offered a helping hand to Judy but she declined and got out on her own.

"I'm starting to get the hang of this," she said proudly.

Paige climbed out carrying a few small packages. The three of them met Tom half way along the dock.

"That's it," he asked, looking at the few packages Paige carried, "After a whole day of shopping?"

Antoinette and Judy only laughed as they walked past him. Paige turned and pointed to where the men were unloading the water taxi, stacking boxes and bags on the dock.

Shaking his head Tom turned to follow the girls.

"Antoinette," he said, "I don't know what Judy told you but that looks like more than half my money back there."

The girls laughed again.

"And how was the fishing?" Judy asked.

"Yeah," added Paige, "Where are the boys?"

"Wait. Wait," Tom said excitedly, "Come here. You have to see this."

Together they hurried to the pier, which was hidden behind the fishing boat. Running ahead, Paige came to a sudden stop.

"Holy cow," she exclaimed.

There stood Tyler and Tommy beaming proud smiles. Behind them was a rack hung with fish. Long silver barracudas, fat tuna, snapper and green Mahi-mahi hung in a row.

Seeing this Judy cheered and Antoinette gasped.

"I will go tell Chef," she said. "Fish for dinner tonight."

Later that day, before dinner, Tyler, Paige, Tommy, Peto and Natalie gathered by the palm trees as they had every day since meeting. Unlike those other days the five of them were not seeing eye-to-eye today. Talk about El Chupacabras had led to an argument.

Tyler pleaded his case.

"But what about last night?" he asked, reminding them again of their nocturnal visit.

"Well, said Paige, "what about it?" She was caught in the middle and was not entirely comfortable being there. Also, she really didn't know what to think about the night before or what she had seen today.

Tyler couldn't believe what he heard.

"What about it," he shouted, "a goatsucker was in our room! And it took the thing we found!"

"Something was in your room," said Natalie. She wasn't ready to admit there was such a thing as a goatsucker.

"Maybe," added Paige, remembering what her parents had said. "And maybe you just lost your thing."

"It was a goatsucker," insisted Tyler, becoming angry.

"And I hit it," added Tommy, "with coconut." For emphasis he held out coconut, which he held in his hand.

There was an angry silence. Tyler glared stubbornly at Natalie, who stared right back.

Not wanting this to ruin what was left of their vacation Paige tried to intervene.

"Let's forget the whole thing."

"Please," Natalie agreed, "it's your last night here, just forget it."

Looking at Natalie—whom he really did like—Tyler was beginning to weaken. He was about to drop the whole thing when Peto spoke up.

"No."

This started Tyler up again.

"What about the ruins?" he argued.

Confused, Natalie quickly asked, "Here? The ruins, here on the island?"

Peto was confused too. He hadn't heard anything about any ruins.

"At that place we went to," Paige explained, "Altun Ha."

Tyler continued. "There was a goatsucker carved into the rock of one of the buildings. It looked just like the one on my...on the necklace."

Tommy turned to Natalie. "What ruins are you talking about?" he asked as the others continued talking about Altun Ha.

"You didn't say anything about that," said Peto.

"I forgot," explained Tyler, "Everything's been happening so fast."

"Natalie," Tommy said, raising his voice. She was trying to ignore him but it was getting difficult.

"The ruins here on the island," she said quietly.

"What ruins?" Tommy asked, surprised.

"Yeah," echoed Peto, who had heard her, "What ruins?"

Now all eyes were on Natalie. She didn't want to say anything but now she had no choice.

"The Rocks. Down at the end of the island."

"The Rocks?" asked Peto, not sure of what he was hearing.

"They're ruins or something. My father said so. He's into that kind of stuff."

"That's it," Peto exclaimed, "That's where we have to look!"

"This is it," said Tyler, "After supper!"

"No," said Paige.

"Yes," said Tyler.

"We can't," Paige said.

"We have to," Tyler insisted.

As they all looked at each other, as if weighing their courage, Peto said, "After supper."

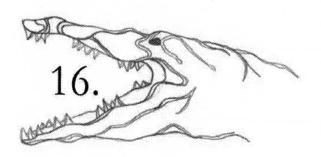

16.

Following a fine fish dinner—and much fussing over Tyler and Tommy, who had caught much of it—Judy and Tom sat in the courtyard outside the cabanas. It wasn't long before the children found them there. They begged and pleaded to be allowed to go play with Peto and Natalie.

Judy explained that they had already had a busy day but they continued. She explained she wanted them rested to travel in the morning but they persisted. Tyler and Paige pleaded while Tommy stood looking sad, cradling coconut in his arms.

"Besides," Paige reasoned, "It is our last night here."

"Why don't you all go swimming," Tom said, offering a compromise.

"Peto and Natalie aren't allowed," said Tyler.

"The pool is for guests," Paige explained. "Please let us go play."

This slowed their parents down. After all, it really wasn't fair. Tom looked at the six sad eyes staring at him.

"Well…" he started, and the children knew they had him. "You know it's alright with me," he said.

All six eyes darted from Tom to Judy. She could feel the pressure on her.

"Alright," she said, relenting to their gaze, "but you know the rules."

"No shenanigans," Tom called after them. With a smile he said to Judy, "It's the only way we'd get any peace."

When they got to the palms Peto and Natalie were already there, only they weren't speaking to each other. The argument had resumed.

Tyler eagerly asked if they were ready. When neither Peto nor Natalie answered he knew something was up.

"I'm not going," Natalie finally said.

Tyler and Tommy looked at her.

"It's stupid," she said, "and dangerous. Can't we just play like normal kids?"

Unable to resist, Tommy teased, "Don't be scurred, coconut will protect you."

Peto laughed along with Tommy.

"Stop it guys," Tyler said. Then, turning to Natalie, he said, "Come on, you can't stay here."

"No, I'm not going," Natalie said again. "I've been there before. You're not going to find anything."

There was a quiet moment as the boys considered what to do. If Natalie stayed there alone, and one of the adults saw her, it might arouse suspicion. On the other hand, this would be their only opportunity to investigate those ruins. And they were sure that this was their chance to catch El Chupacabras.

"I'll stay with Natalie," Paige said. "She's right you know, you aren't going to find anything there."

"You sure?" Tyler asked Paige.

Paige nodded as Natalie turned away. Paige followed her.

"You know you can go with them," said Natalie when Paige caught up with her. "I mean I wouldn't tell if anyone asked where you guys were."

"That's okay," Paige assured her. "You're right, they're not going to find anything there."

"It's not that I'm scared or anything like that," said Natalie, "But my dad, he wants to stay here and maybe get a chance to run a resort some day. So, I really can't get into any trouble."

"That's okay, you don't have to explain," said Paige. Then she confided to Natalie, "I think it was Reaux who stole the necklace anyway, not any chupacabras."

"Why?"

Paige went on to explain how she had spotted Reaux in town and what she had seen.

"Did you tell Tyler?" Natalie asked.

"No, he wouldn't believe me anyway," said Paige. "He wants to believe in the goatsucker instead."

Tyler, Tommy and Peto emerged from a seldom-used path. Peto carried a small canvas bag. Tommy carried coconut.

"This is it," said Peto.

'The Rocks' were just that, a pile of weathered rock on the water's edge at the island's north tip. But despite their age, and haphazard appearance, it was obvious that at some time the rocks must have been cut and placed there. They still had the square, chunky look of a Mayan pyramid.

"What is it?" Tommy asked.

"I guess it was a pyramid," said Tyler, "Come on." He led the others to the rocks. There wasn't much time. Already long shadows were reaching from the jungle to the rocks as the sun set over the lagoons.

Tommy and Peto climbed the rocks while Tyler walked around them.

"Hey," Tommy asked, "What are we looking for?"

Tyler shrugged and looked up at Peto.

"Some sign of chupacabras," said Peto.

"Like what?" asked Tommy, "Chupa poopa?"

Peto and Tyler looked at Tommy, telling him to be serious.

"Just asking," he said.

"Like tracks or something," Peto said. "Or clues," Tyler added.

After scouring the entire area, they sat on the rocks. It looked as if Natalie was right, they found nothing of interest. And now the shadows were climbing over the rocks and reaching to the water.

Sitting above Peto and his brother, Tommy spun coconut on its end as he listened to the older boys.

"Now what," said Tyler, "we have to be back by dark."

"Let's go," said Peto, disappointed.

"Where do you think these rocks came from?" Tyler asked as they stood to leave. But before Peto could venture a guess Tommy bumped the spinning coconut. It rolled and bounced down the rocks. At the bottom it rolled off the low edge, splashing into the water. It bobbed to the surface then disappeared.

Tommy started down after it but Peto stopped him.

"Wait, I'll get it."

Peto lowered himself and lay face down on the lowest rock, expecting to be able to reach coconut from there. Looking to the water, he was surprised not to see it.

"Did it sink?" Tyler suggested.

"No, they float," said Peto. "Wait," he said, as he stretched further out over the water. "Come here."

"Do you see coconut?" Tommy asked anxiously.

"No, but I can see under the rocks."

"What?" they said in disbelief. They were amazed.

Without warning Peto rolled off the rock and into the water. When he surfaced he was standing shoulder deep in the water.

"There's a cave here," he announced.

17.

Peto stood in the water peering into the cave.

Where the rocks met the water there was a gap of about one foot above the water. This gap extended below the water as well. Reaching out, Peto couldn't feel any obstructions. Deciding there was only one way to see where this opening led he stepped forward and into the cave.

Watching from the rocks above Tyler was speechless. Excited by the possibilities Tommy tugged at his brother's arm.

"Remember what the man said."

"What man?" asked Tyler.

"The man at the pyramid," Tommy said, "He said the Maya built their stuff on top of each other."

Peto stepped back out from under the rocks.

"Get my bag," he said, pointing to the bag he had carried with him.

Tyler scrambled over the pyramid and brought the bag back to the edge of the overhanging rock. Dangling it out over the water he held it while Peto dug a small flashlight out.

Peto paused and looked up at his friends.

"Come on."

Tossing Peto's bag aside Tyler jumped into the water. Tommy hesitated, but followed. Tommy was nearly a head shorter than and Tyler had to bounce on his toes to keep his head above water.

One after another they disappeared into the opening.

"Coconut," Tommy exclaimed. His voice bounced about the cave. Following the beam of Peto's flashlight, Tommy saw that coconut was only one of many floating in the cave. "Wow," he said, "it's a coconut family reunion."

Along with the coconuts the surface of the water was crowded with floating debris. Lost fishing gear, wood, and plastic bottles all rode the gentle rise and fall of the water, making a chattering sound as they rubbed against one another.

Walking into the cave the boys were glad to feel the floor sloping upward. Soon they were only waist deep in water.

Peto shined the light about the cave. It was the size of a small room and just tall enough for them to stand upright in.

Peto said, "There is more."

Past the *flotsam* on the water the floor of the cave could be seen rising out of the water. Walking past Tyler and Tommy, Peto waded through everything, leading the way further into the cave.

Tyler and Peto used the flashlight to explore. Tommy, though at first intrigued, was becoming increasingly uncomfortable and stayed near the water's edge.

There was little to see in the cave, just sand and rock floor and a low rocky ceiling. Then they noticed how the light played on the cave walls. It seemed to shine and almost glitter in places. They took the flashlight closer, feeling the stone in places and moving the light back and forth over it.

"What is it?" asked Tyler.

"Coral," said Peto, "I think it is coral. And very old coral. The kind used for jewelry"

"Wait," said Tyler, noticing something else. He grabbed Peto's hand and redirected the flashlight's beam.

"Look," he said, "It looks like jade. I bet this is where the necklace came from."

"Come on. Let's go," said Tommy as Tyler and Peto examined more of the walls.

"There's more," said Peto from the farthest corner of the room. He had discovered that the cave seemed to go on. Tyler hurried over and the two of them looked into a craggy crack in the wall. Indeed, it seemed to go on but it was not at all inviting.

"Come on," said Tommy again, "It was getting dark out."

Turning to look at Tommy, Peto bumped something with his foot. "Hey, look at this."

From just inside the dark opening he picked up an old geologist hammer, the type with a pick on one side and a blunt hammer on the other.

"It looks pretty old," he said looking at it. The hammer's wooden handle was rough and the metal parts rusted but the tip of the pick, as well as the face of the hammer, were clean and rust free.

"Look at this too," said Tyler, spotting an old, well-used chisel nearby.

"Well," said Peto, "we're not the first ones here."

"No. This place must have been a mine or something," Tyler suggested.

"Come on," said Tommy, with some fear in his voice, "I want to get out of here."

"Well, let's go this way," said Peto, shining the light into the crack in the wall. "Maybe it goes out."

"Who knows if it goes anywhere," said Tyler, "We'd better go out the way we came." He knew his brother was afraid and would never go through the narrow passage. He was becoming uncomfortable too.

Back at the water's edge it seemed that the water has risen. Peto shined the light toward the opening.

"The hole is smaller," said Tommy, panic in his voice.

"The tide is rising," Peto explained.

The lap of the water on the rocks and the chatter of the debris in the water echoed in the cave, sounding menacing and *claustrophobic*. Feeling his brother's fear, Tyler put his arm around Tommy.

"Don't worry," he assured him, "we can still walk right out."

"Are you sure?"

"Just follow me," said Peto.

At the mouth of the cave Tommy was already on his tiptoes struggling to keep his head above water. "I can't," he said, spitting out water, "It's too deep."

"Sure you can," Tyler insisted, "Come here."

Pulling his younger brother between Peto and himself, the two of them held Tommy up enough to keep his head above water. Confident now, they took a few steps forward. Then Peto stopped.

"Sssshhh," he said.

Standing still, with Tommy between them, they listened. Soon they managed to make out the sound of an outboard motor. It seemed to be approaching.

Through what was left of the opening a boat came into view. It was the snorkeling boat from Journey's End. It seemed to be coming their way but as it neared The Rocks it didn't slow down. Wondering what would happen the boys took a step back.

Just when it seemed that the boat would run into the rocks it turned hard and the engine stopped. For just a second the boys could see Felix at the controls. Then the wave from the boat's wake rolled through the opening, swamping the boys and sending them reeling backwards in the water.

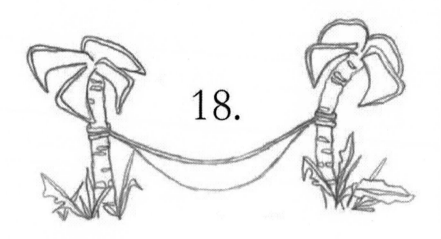

18.

With the boys off exploring Journey's End was very quiet. Paige and Natalie wandered about a bit before settling in a hammock in a secluded corner. There they talked quietly.

"So you take a boat to school too," said Paige.

Natalie nodded. Paige had been quizzing her on what it was like to live there all the time.

"It's pretty cool," she said. "The kids there are from all over and there's a lot of them so the teacher is usually pretty busy. She let's me do my own work or help her."

"Wait," said Paige, "'the teacher', there is one teacher, for all the grades, for the whole school?"

Natalie nodded again. She had forgotten how different life here was from other places. She was enjoying telling Paige about it.

Paige was about to ask more when Natalie held her finger to her lips and whispered, "What was that?"

"What?"

"I thought I heard something," said Natalie, pointing to the bushes behind them.

The two of them scrunched down in the hammock, peeking over its edge. After a few seconds of this they began squirming and the hammock began to swing.

Again there was a noise. This time they both heard it. It sounded like something making its way through the brush.

They stretched to see it.

They stretched some more.

They squealed as the hammock tipped, spilling them on to the ground. They lie in the sand giggling until Natalie pointed.

"There they go."

"Who?"

"I don't know," said Natalie, "but I saw feet. Come on."

Natalie jumped up and set off after whoever it was. Paige was too slow to stop her. With a sigh, she followed.

Natalie slinked along, following whoever it was. In the twilight Paige followed along the shadowy and unfamiliar path. Though she wasn't sure where they were she trusted her friend.

Natalie slowed, then stopped. Paige came up behind her.

"It's Reaux," Natalie whispered in her ear.

But before Paige could even breath, Natalie was off again. With another sigh Paige followed.

The next time she stopped Natalie seemed confused. Standing beside her Paige tried to look into the darkness.

"Where did he go?"

"I don't know," Natalie answered.

Seeing nothing that looked familiar, something else occurred to Paige. "Ahh…" she asked, "Where are we?"

"Near the end of the island, I guess," Natalie said.

"Near The Rocks?"

"Pretty close, I guess."

Thinking of Tyler, Tommy and Peto, Paige knew she would feel much better if they were all together. "Let's see if they are still there," she suggested.

Natalie quickly agreed but before they had taken more than three steps they realized something was behind them.

They heard the hissing growl of the chupacabras before looking.

Crouching in the shadows the goatsucker stared out at them, its long red eyes just about lost in the dark.

It hissed again. The bushes shook as it lunged forward, threatening the girls.

They screamed then ran.

19.

"Which way?"

In the dark, silent jungle Paige's voice sounded small and alone.

"I don't know," said Natalie.

In their panic the girls had abandoned the path they had been on and lost their sense of direction. Now they were afraid of becoming separated as well.

Holding hands, they picked their way through the brush.

"It doesn't matter," Natalie reasoned, "just keep going and we'll wind up somewhere."

"Somewhere?"

"Back on the path, the shore, The Rocks—somewhere," said Natalie, "It's an island."

Paige tugged at her hand.

"What about the...?"

"We can't stay here," was all Natalie said. She pulled Paige along. "Come on. Watch out for this log here."

Reluctantly, Paige stepped over the log and followed Natalie until she stopped again. Natalie backed up against her. Something was coming through the bushes right in front of them.

All Paige could see was the outline of something ducking under a tree limb. It had a *crest* or something sticking up on its head.

The girls began retreating in fear even though it didn't seem to see them. They had already forgotten about the log. With a shriek they tumbled over it.

Startled by their shrieks, it jumped. Crab-walking back across the sand they heard a voice.

"No," it said, "No mon."

They crawled even further away.

"It is me," it said, "Chef."

As it came closer they saw that it was Chef, without his hat and with his dreadlocks up, come looking for them.

"Chef," Natalie finally cried out, overjoyed to see his friendly face.

"I heard screaming," said Chef.

Just now catching her breath, Paige joined in. "We thought you were a goatsucker."

"What are you doing out here," Chef asked.

Getting up off the ground, the girls stepped into Chef's safe arms. Feeling their fear he stopped his questioning to comfort them. Until he realized what Paige had said.

"You thought I was a what girl?"

"A chupacabras," Paige said, a little embarrassed to admit it now.

Chef rolled his eyes, "No, not that again."

A few minutes later Chef had the girls calmed down. Standing there in the dark he told them it was time to go, it was no place for children and their parents would be worried.

"Come along," he said, carefully picking his way through the brush. He would take the girls to his home then return them to Journey's End.

"Something scared you yes," he said to them, "but what were you doing out here at night?"

"We were following Reaux," said Natalie, "he was…"

"Reaux?"

Chef was surprised to hear that. Everyone knew that Reaux did not come out at night.

"Then we thought of the boys," Paige added.

"The boys?" said Chef, "What of the boys?"

"They went to The Rocks," the girls explained.

"The Rocks? Oh mon, why The Rocks?"

"Well," Natalie began, "Tyler found this necklace, a Mayan one, with a chupa on it."

"And then," Paige continued, "at the pyramids he saw a carving in a rock…"

Chef shook his head.

"Oh these stories," he said.

He told the girls they had best go to The rocks and check on the boys. As he changed direction and led them that way, the girls continued chattering behind him, telling him all that had been going on.

20.

The cave was dark and getting cold.

The rising tide had blocked the opening that the boys had come in through, cutting off any light or fresh air from that direction. The flashlight was their only light and that was beginning to fade.

Peto pointed it toward the opening of the cave one more time then turned to his companions. Tommy was frightened and clung to his brother. And Tyler had the look of someone who only now realized they were in over their heads.

"We can still swim out," Peto said.

Tommy shook his head no.

Tyler wasn't convinced either. Beside, he knew that no amount of convincing would get Tommy to try.

"Well," said Peto, "the light won't last."

Tyler nodded his head toward the back of the cave. "Maybe there's another way out," he suggested. He was thinking of the passage Peto had spotted earlier.

"We can look," Peto said.

Carefully they made their way back to where they had been earlier. Tyler held his brother's hand, assuring him all the while that all would be well.

Finding the crack in the cave wall, Peto turned sideways and slid into it. Tommy watched, coconut under his arm.

Tyler gave him a little nudge from behind.

"Go ahead, I'll be right behind you."

Peto stepped back out so that Tommy could see him.

"It's alright," Peto said.

"Come on buddy," said Tyler, "let's take a look. It's probably just like *Crystal Caves* back home. Remember?"

With this Tommy got his nerve up. He nodded to Peto. Proud of him Tyler mussed his hair.

One by one they squeezed into the fissure and were swallowed by the dark.

21.

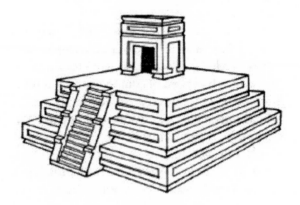

All was quiet at The Rocks. Even the lap of the water was subdued.

Felix sat on the rocks looking out over the water, one foot on the boat so it wouldn't bump the rocks and make noise. He had been there some time listening and waiting where he could not be seen.

Finally, the quiet was broken by several voices. This was not what Felix expected. Only one person was supposed to come. He hid.

On the other side of the rocks, Chef, Natalie and Paige emerged from the brush. Stopping, they looked about and listened.

Chef turned and spoke to the girls.

"There is no one here."

Paige called out hesitantly, almost afraid of disturbing the quiet.

"Tyler? Tommy?"

"Peto? Tyler?" called Natalie, louder.

They walked to The Rocks and Chef followed.

"They're not here," he said as they climbed the rocks. "Careful there," he warned.

Paige moved around the rocks toward the other side.

"Hey," she called back, "there's a boat here."

"What?" said Chef, surprised yet again at the things he was finding in the night.

"A boat," Paige repeated.

Natalie hurried to Paige. As she did she tripped over something.

By now Chef had climbed onto the rocks as well. He helped Natalie to her feet.

"Here's Peto's bag," she said, holding it up. "They were here."

"What is going on here?" Chef wondered aloud.

While Chef stood and pondered, trying to piece things together, Paige and Natalie called out the boy's names, hoping for an answer.

They kept this up for quite some time, but it became obvious that wherever they were, the boys couldn't hear them. Chef sat by the boat, wondering how it had got there.

Then they heard it—a quiet voice calling from the brush. Thinking it must be her brothers Paige jumped from the rocks and ran toward it. Natalie chased after her.

Chef jumped to his feet as well. He was about to warn them to stop but as the words were leaving his lips he suddenly and unnaturally went silent.

Holding the girls by their wrists Reaux dragged them from the jungle to the boat. Near The Rocks they passed Chef lying unconscious on the ground. Felix knelt over him, tying his hands behind his back with a scrap of rope.

Seeing Chef the girls gasped.

They struggled to pull free and get to their injured friend but Reaux held tight, pulling them away.

Struggling with the girls, he called back to Felix.

"That's good. Come on."

Reaux pushed the girls toward the boat. Once they were in it Felix stood over them, making sure they didn't try to escape. After seeing Chef lying bound and motionless in the sand they were too frightened to even think of it.

Reaux disappeared into the darkness for a moment. When he reappeared he was carrying two heavy sacks. Carefully he handed them down to Felix in the boat.

22.

Out in the jungle a pale light appeared behind a bush. It moved, becoming brighter, though not too bright.

A voice could be heard.

"This is it! This is it! I can see leaves and stuff!"

It was Peto.

The bush moved—first just the branches, then the entire thing.

Peto stepped out from behind it.

"Someone was keeping this hidden," he said to Tyler and Tommy who emerged behind him.

They had been right. After its tight narrow beginning in the cave under the rocks, the passage had opened up enough to crawl through. After what seemed like twenty miles, but was probably more like twenty yards, it rose to the surface. That was where they had climbed out behind that bush.

All three stretched, glad to be out of the confines of the cave.

"I wonder what time it is?" said Tyler.

"Come on," said Tommy, "let's just get back."

Then they heard the boat's motor start. They had forgotten all about Felix and the boat.

"Come on," Peto cried out.

The three of them ran to the sound and found themselves back at The Rocks.

The boat was just pulling away.

"Hold on!" called Peto, "*Esperar!*"

"Hey! Wait!" Tyler yelled.

On the boat Natalie excitedly waved her arms.

"Peto," she called out, "we're on the boat!"

Paige yelled also.

"Help! Tyler! It's Reaux," she said, hoping that Tyler would know what she meant.

The girls continued yelling but their voices were overpowered by the boat's motor.

In a panic Tyler ran to the shore.

"Paige," he yelled, "Paige wait!

Peto joined him. Together they watched as the boat sped off. In the light of the rising moon they could just make out the figures of the men standing over the girls in the boat.

They stood speechless.

"Tyler," Tommy called out, panic in his voice. "Tyler!"

Tyler and Peto looked at each other. They hadn't even realized that Tommy wasn't with them. Turning, they saw him standing near The Rocks and ran to him.

He was standing over a still body.

"It's Chef," said Peto.

"Is he dead?" Tommy asked.

"Dead?" said Tyler, frightened. He had not even thought of that.

"Dead?" said Chef as he awoke. His voice was slow and groggy.

Stunned, the boys stared down at him.

"No mon, I am not dead," Chef said. "Help me up."

Relieved, the boys were only too eager to help Chef to his feet, but he immediately sat down again. He had been hit on the head and was still feeling it.

"The girls?" Chef asked, "Where are the girls?"

"They went…" Peto started, "They took them, in a boat."

"Reaux—that rat—and someone else," said Chef, "Someone who hit me."

"Felix," said Peto to Chef. "You know, the one who runs the boat. He was here with the boat before."

Impatiently Tyler spoke up.

"Come on. We have to go get them, Paige and Natalie."

"Where did they go?" asked Tommy.

There was silence then Chef looked at Peto.

"I think I know," he said.

"Rattan?" Peto asked, sure that this is the answer.

"Rattan," said Chef.

23.

The four of them—Peto, Tyler, Tommy and Chef—hurried to the resort to get help. They would go on to Rattan from there. Although Chef's head injury slowed them down they soon were on the beach by the palms.

Chef stopped the boys there, telling them he must tell their parents what was happening before going any further.

"No," Tyler protested, "we can't wait."

"We have to save Paige and Natalie," Tommy cried, hugging coconut to his chest.

"We must tell them," Chef argued.

"No, we have to hurry," Tyler shot back.

Chef pointed.

"Look, there's Antoinette. Just let me tell her."

Without thinking what the boys might do Chef started off to where he had seen the waitress.

"Let's go," said Tyler, leading Peto and Tommy into the dark as soon as Chef's back was turned.

"Hey! Get back here!" Chef yelled after them.

Unable to run after them, he called out to Antoinette.

Rattan was near by, closer than the boys had thought, but with the girls in danger and all that had happened it felt like they had been running forever. By the time they came to the abandoned resort the boys were *winded* and their feet ached from running on the sand.

Staying out of the open they scanned the buildings there, hoping to quickly spot someone.

"There is the boat," Peto whispered, pointing to the unfinished dock. The boat was tied there.

This meant they were right. Reaux and Felix had brought the girls to Rattan.

"Where are they?' Tommy asked impatiently.

"Ssshhhh," Tyler said, silencing his brother. He turned to Peto, "Have you ever been here?"

"Si," said Peto, "I am not supposed to come here, but I have visited once or twice."

"Where could they be?" Tommy asked again.

"There."

Peto pointed to the main building. Tyler realized that this was the building that he had seen from the water when passing by. This was the building that was shaped like a squat pyramid and had a glass front.

A dim light could be seen through the building's glass block *façade*. It moved. It was a flashlight moving inside.

Coconut in hand, Tommy took off toward the building.

"Hey, get back here," Tyler called out in a loud whisper. It did no good; Tommy kept going.

Tyler went after him, Peto followed.

The three of them ducked down below the low wall that ran along the top of the steps. From there they could see the light much better. They could also see through the front doorways, which were open and without doors.

"We can't go in that way, they'll see us," said Peto, taking charge. "There is a back door."

Eager to rescue Natalie and Paige, Tommy and Tyler stood up. Peto pulled them back down.

"One at a time," he said. Checking to make sure the coast was clear he nudged Tyler. "Go."

Tyler scooted across the patio and past the doorways. When he turned to look back, Peto signaled him to go behind the building and wait.

Turning to Tommy, Peto said, "Your turn."

Tommy crept past the doorways on tiptoes. Once he was past them he turned to go behind the building. Then he dropped coconut. The sound it made rang out like a gunshot.

Tommy froze.

Peto watched coconut roll onto the patio.

They held their breath and watched as the beam of the flashlight poked out of the doorway.

Felix stepped out from the doorway and looked around. He shined the light on coconut then around the patio, just missing Tommy who stood on his toes like a statue. Felix shined his light into the trees, then back on coconut.

"Nothing," he called back into the building, "Just a coconut."

He went back inside.

Peto waited before running across the patio, stooping to pick up coconut along the way. Pushing coconut into Tommy's hands he pulled him along.

Joining Tyler behind the building, Tommy looked at his brother and said, "Did you see coconut play dead?"

Tyler gave him a slap in the head as Peto pointed out the back door and led them to it.

Inside, Peto led them up a short dark hall. Stopping at the end of it the boys could see into the lobby where they had seen the light.

There were Natalie and Paige, sitting back to back on the floor. Their wrists were tied together, keeping them that way.

Reaux stood near one of the doorways. On the floor near him were several sacks similar to the ones he had loaded onto the boat earlier.

"We'll take these with us," he was saying, "they're worth enough to keep us happy for a while."

Felix came from another room carrying two more sacks.

"Is that all?" Reaux asked.

"No, there is one more," answered Felix.

He paused and looked at the girls.

"What about them?" he asked.

Peto, Tyler and Tommy could see the girls looking up at their captors with terror in their eyes.

Reaux looked at the girls then leaned closer to Felix.

"We'll take them with us and drop them somewhere where they won't be found," he said and winked.

Felix watched the girl's faces. Seeing their fear he laughed.

"The crocs, huh," he laughed, "That's good."

He laughed even more as the girls struggled to look at each other.

Shocked by what they had heard the boys looked at each other in panic. Remembering the crocodile's hot breath on his face, Tommy nearly cried out.

Still laughing, Felix went to get the last sack.

Peto led Tommy and Tyler back down the hall, away from Reaux and the girls.

"We have to do something," said Tyler.

"Stop them," said Tommy, beginning to panic.

Peto thought for a few seconds.

"Okay," he said, "I'll take care of the boat. You two watch them."

About to leave, he stopped.

"Don't worry," he said soothingly to Tommy, "Chef will be here soon. We just have to slow them down"

Peto left.

Tyler and Tommy exchanged worried looks as they made their way back up the hall. As they watched, Reaux prepared to leave. After first making sure his young *accomplice* wasn't back yet, he rooted through one of the sacks took out several large pieces of jade for himself and stuffed them into his pockets.

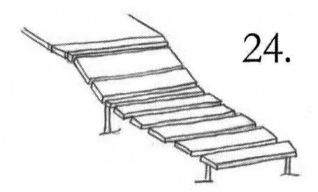

24.

Peto approached the dock.

By now the moon had risen and he had some light to work in. He crept out onto the dock and *contemplated* the boat.

'How to *sabotage* the boat?' He asked himself.

He patted his pockets, looking for something to use. All he had was a small pocketknife. Taking it out, he opened it. He looked at the boat then at the little knife in his hand.

He lowered himself into the boat.

He was still trying to think of something to do when he heard Felix come out of the building. Peto could see him coming his way carrying several sacks.

As Felix came onto the dock Peto eased himself over the edge of the boat and into the water; when Felix got near the boat he slid out of sight.

After he put the sacks into the boat, Felix stood on the dock and looked back down the beach. He could just make out some small lights moving on the beach.

Knowing what that meant he ran back to the building. When he did Peto reappeared at the side of the boat. Gripping his knife in his teeth like a pirate he climbed back in.

Feeling helpless, Tommy and Tyler watched as Reaux pulled the girls to their feet. He was ready to leave when Felix rushed back in.

"Hurry," he said, "They are coming up the beach."

"Who is coming?"

"I don't know who," explained Felix, "but there is a lot of them."

"Everything is ready, we'll be gone when they get here," Reaux said confidently.

Taking all they could carry, they hurried out, pushing the girls ahead of them.

Out on the patio the girls tried to run, only to fall on the steps. Still tied together they couldn't get up.

Felix laughed as Reaux roughly pulled them to their feet again and dragged them to the boat.

Putting the girls in the boat, Felix forced them to sit on the wet floor. He then went to the back of the boat to start the motor. Reaux stood ready to untie the boat. Felix set the motor and was about to pull the starter when he stopped.

"Come on," said Reaux, looking at the approaching lights, "Let's go."

"It's gone," said Felix, looking at the motor, "The thing, it's gone."

"What's gone?" asked Reaux impatiently.

"The thing," Felix stammered, not knowing what to call it. Trying to explain he *pantomimed* pulling the rope to start the engine. "Handle. Rope. It's gone."

Looking quite *inept*, Felix began looking on the bottom of the boat, as if it might be found lying there. Still tied back to back, with Paige, Natalie could see what was happening, Paige could not. She could only watch as Reaux looked to the approaching lights.

"You look for your rope," said Reaux angrily, "I am not going to be caught here looking like a fool."

Reaching into one of the sacks Reaux pulled out a *sheath*. From the sheath he pulled a gleaming knife.

Paige was petrified as Reaux came toward her and Natalie, knife in hand. He pulled the two of them up and cut the rope that bound them together. Separating them he pushed Natalie back into Felix. The two of them fell in a heap in the back of the boat.

Pulling Paige by the wrist, Reaux climbed onto the dock. There Peto stood. He meant to stop Reaux even though all he had was his little pocketknife.

"Peto no," Paige yelled.

Reaux swung at the boy with his knife and Peto fell back off the edge of the dock.

"Peto," Paige yelled again as she was pulled away. Reaux dragged her along as he ran up the steps and onto the patio.

On the patio Tyler and Tommy ran from where they were hiding to try and stop Reaux. As always it was Tommy who led the charge.

"No Tommy," Paige cried, "Don't!"

As Tommy faced Reaux Tyler came up behind his brother.

"Tyler stop Tommy," Paige said, "Reaux has a knife!"

Tyler grabbed his brother but they didn't retreat.

"You're not taking our sister," Tyler said to Reaux.

Reaux waved the knife menacingly.

"But I have the knife little boy," he teased, "what about that?"

Reaux took a quick poke at Tommy with the knife. Unharmed, Tommy flinched then charged at Reaux.

Reaux stabbed at Tommy again. This time his thrust hit home, pushing Tommy back into Tyler's arms. Unable to pull the knife loose, Reaux let go and left it behind.

Paige screamed as Reaux dragged her away.

Pushed back onto the ground Tyler held Tommy in his arms. Something dripped onto his legs.

"Tommy?" Tyler said, desperately wanting to hear his brother's voice, "Tommy?"

"Oh no," said Tommy surprised and scared.

"Are you...?" Tyler began to ask, fearing the worst. "Are you alright?"

Tommy held coconut up in the moonlight. Reaux's knife was stuck in it. Coconut milk dripped onto the two of them.

25.

Back in the boat Felix struggled with Natalie. She wasn't about to let him go without a fight but the older boy quickly won out. Leaving her behind he decided to follow Reaux and ran down the dock but as he reached the shore Peto came running up out of the water. Throwing himself at Felix as hard as he could Peto tackled him, throwing him down face first in the sand.

From on the dock Natalie cheered for Peto then came running to help. Together the two of them wrestled with Felix and managed to hold his face in the sand until voices could be heard approaching.

Lights soon illuminated them as they grappled on the beach. Felix stopped struggling and surrendered when he saw he was surrounded.

By the time Felix surrendered on the beach Reaux had dragged Paige into the jungle. They were on a path she hadn't seen before but if she were right he was taking her back toward The Rocks. She fought and struggled, trying to slow him down, but he was unrelenting.

"Come with me," he said, "or I'll do you like I did your brother."

This scared Paige and she stopped fighting for a moment. "Poor Tommy," she thought, "he was only trying to protect her." She hoped he was all right. Knowing that she could only help him if she could get back to him, she renewed her efforts to escape.

After a few minutes of this she began to tire. Then they came to a spot on the path that looked familiar.

"Of course," she thought, realizing where they were. "This was where Peto had his chupacabras trap."

Now she fought harder than ever, slowly pulling Reaux toward the hidden trap. Tugging and pulling she brought him ever closer, half a step at a time.

Finally, he stepped on the trap.

Nothing happened.

Paige looked.

Reaux had only one foot on the trap. Paige *lunged* out, pulling his arm then turned, forcing him to put both feet on the trap—hard.

The trap gave way and Reaux fell into the pit. His weight began to pull Paige with him but she managed not to fall in. Letting out a pained scream Reaux released his grip on her wrist.

Breathing heavy, Paige rolled away. Behind her Reaux's hand grasped at the trap's remaining timbers. His head began to reappear and then, with another pained scream, it dropped from sight.

Startled by this second scream, Paige scrambled to her feet and ran.

Paige hadn't gone very far when she met her brothers coming to find her.

"You're okay," she beamed, seeing Tommy coming to her rescue. She scooped him up and gave him a big hug.

"Where is he?" Tyler asked, intent on finding Reaux.

"In the trap!" said Paige, "Peto's trap got him. And I think he's hurt."

"Then let's make sure he doesn't get away," said Tyler.

"Let's get him," said Tommy.

Nearing the trap the children slowed down. The bravery they felt a moment ago was fading fast. After all, this was a man who had tried to stab Tommy, and who had been planning to leave Paige and Natalie to the crocodiles.

"He sounded like he was hurt," whispered Paige.

"There's the trap," said Tyler, pointing to the broken boards.

Unsure of themselves, they backed up a bit.

Without a word Tommy looked to the ground and picked up a stick. Tyler did the same.

Sticks held ready the boys approached the trap.

"Is he there?" Paige asked.

"I can't see," answered Tyler.

He stepped up and hit what was left of the trap with his stick. When the board he hit collapsed back into the hole all three of them jumped.

Nothing more happened and again they *gingerly* crept up. Cautiously, they peeked into the hole.

"He's gone," Tommy announced.

Paige looked down the path.

"This way."

"Wait," said Tyler, "What's this?"

He stopped and picked up something near the trap. It was a pair of glasses, red wrap around glasses with red reflective lenses. Tyler turned them over in his hand then held them up to look through.

Paige and Tommy gasped.

"Goatsucker glasses," Paige whispered.

"Hurry," Tommy said, "He'll get away."

Moments later they caught up with Reaux on the path. In pain, he was limping but still intent on getting away. With his stick in hand, Tommy was ready to go at him but Tyler stopped him. He knew how dangerous Reaux could be.

"Wait," he said to his brother, an idea forming in his head. "Paige, come here."

26.

Reaux limped along the dark path. He hadn't seen or heard anyone since climbing out of that hole but still he hurried, cursing the injury that slowed him down.

He was still confident he could find a place to hide for the night and escape in the morning.

"Perhaps in the cave," he was thinking, "I could hide there for the night."

As far as he knew that was still a secret. Then he thought he heard something.

First it sounded as if it were along the path to the right, then it seemed to be to the left. It sounded almost as if someone were running through the brush along the path.

He stopped.

The noise stopped.

Peering into the jungle he thought something stared back.

Wanting only to hide and rest his injured ankle Reaux started along the path again, picking up the pace this time. He winced in pain every time he put his left foot down.

The sounds began again. Nervously he watched the jungle around him. Thinking he heard a hissing he stopped again. Straining to see in the dark he tried to figure out what was happening.

When he turned his attention back to the path someone—no, something—poked its head out and showed fangs.

Startled, he jumped, hurting his ankle even more.

The head he had seen disappeared.

"You won't scare me," Reaux yelled, shaking his fist at the jungle.

He had only taken a few steps when something ran across the path behind him, hissing as it went. When he turned to look he fell. As he tried to get up something sharp and dry poked at his back, first on one side, then on the other.

Off in the jungle he heard an awful hiss and then another off in the other direction.

"No," he told himself, "No, it's not real."

As if to convince himself he repeated the thought out loud. Taking long, deep breaths he calmed himself enough to get to his feet and start off again.

Struggling along the path the harassment continued—hissing noises all around him, poking and grabbing. Once, something grabbed at his foot, tripping him. He had to crawl to escape.

Finally, he was in so much pain, and so distracted, that he took a wrong turn, turning to where the children had seen the crocodiles. When he did what had been following him came out of the jungle and crossed the path—smiling as it did.

It was Paige with her hair down over her face and Tyler's fangs in her mouth! She wore the red glasses they had found. Tommy and Tyler came out behind her carrying the long sticks they had been using to poke and trip Reaux.

Reaux limped forward as fast as he could until he saw the lagoon. A crocodile splashed in front of him. Realizing he was well off the path he stopped.

When he turned around to retrace his steps Paige jumped out at him and hissed. This time Reaux saw through her disguise and charged at her. Seeing he was no longer fooled Paige retreated. Just when it seemed that the furious Reaux would get her Tyler and Tommy managed to trip him up.

He lay sprawled in the sand. Rolling over all he could see was sky above. But he could hear voices, adult voices, nearby. He rolled back onto his belly and hugged the ground like a snake, hoping to hide.

All was quiet.

He waited. And waited.

Just when he was beginning to think that he still might have a chance something came down hard on his left ankle. He screamed out in pain.

As the beam of a flashlight found him he heard Tommy say, "That's for coconut!"

Reaux lie on the ground as if pinned there by the light that shined on him.

"Here he is," a voice called out, "We got him."

"The children? Are the children there?" Judy's voice asked from a distance.

More light shone on the scene, finding the children surrounding Reaux. Tommy, Paige and Tyler recognized the people gathering around them. The lights lingered on Paige in her disguise.

"Yes," one of the people yelled back, "they're here."

Chef stepped up to check on his young friends. Quickly seeing the situation he laughed loudly, "Oh yeah, they are here mon. And it looks like they got him."

Reaux began to stir, thinking of making one last try at escaping. Chef pointed and wagged his finger.

"No, no. Don't you get up."

Tom and Judy rushed onto the scene. Looking down at Reaux they carefully stepped around him and hurried to the children.

Looking at Paige, Judy gasped.

"What on earth?" she started to say, "What happened to you?"

Paige hissed then laughed, "M'm a shuba…" She tried speaking but the fangs were in the way.

Laughing more she dropped the fangs into her hand and said, "I'm a chupaca-bras."

27.

By the time breakfast was finished the following morning it was time for the Olivers to be going. The excitement of the night had eased somewhat, the luggage was packed and stacked by the cabana doors and an empty cart stood ready to carry it to the dock.

Antoinette and Peto stood in the courtyard with Tom, Judy, Tyler, Paige and Tommy. As they began saying their farewells Natalie and her father came along. Letting go of her father's hand Natalie ran to Paige.

"Guess what," she said excitedly, "My dad is in charge."

"Really?" said Paige, "That's so cool."

She was excited for her friend.

Coming up behind her Bert tried to explain, "Temporarily, Natalie. That means…"

"I know what it means Dad," she said, "Still, I'm so proud of you."

"Yeah, that's great," said Tom, shaking Bert's hand.

"It's about time," Antoinette agreed.

Paige tugged at Natalie's hand, pulling her to the cabana. "Come here," she said as she pulled her inside.

There she went directly to the nightstand and picked up a small bag. From the bag she brought out two necklaces she had bought in the city.

"Here. One is for you and one is mine."

"Thanks," said Natalie as she hugged her friend. "It's so pretty.

"It's to remind you of me," said Paige, "and my brothers."

"I don't think I'll ever forget you, or your family" Natalie laughed.

Outside the cabanas Tyler was talking to Natalie's father. Both were excited about what the boys had found under The Rocks.

"I don't think any actual Mayan mines have ever been found," Bert was saying, "so that's a first."

"Do you think that's where the jade head—Kinich Ahau—came from?" Tyler asked. He imagined being famous for finding the elusive source of that huge piece of jade.

"That's for the experts to say," said Bert, not wanting to speculate. "No matter what though, it has to be a special and sacred place."

While they were talking Chef strolled into the courtyard. Tommy ran to him.

"Hey little mon," Chef greeted him.

"Hey big mon," said Tommy, imitating his Jamaican friend.

Tom, Judy and Antoinette gathered around Chef.

"Well?" said Tom.

"Well," announced Chef, "Reaux is gone. The authorities have removed him."

"That's a relief," said Judy.

"Who took him?" Tommy asked.

"The mon came and took him away mon," Chef said with a grin. "I ask them to take you too but they say, 'No room in the boat mon.'"

Tommy laughed as Chef poked his chest and messed with his hair.

Antoinette sighed.

"What was it Reaux was doing?" she asked, "I still don't understand."

"He was taking coral and jade from that cave Felix found and selling it," Chef explained. "You are not supposed to do that. Especially from a site like The Rocks."

"So what was with the stories?" Antoinette asked.

"Yeah," said Tommy, "What about the goatsucker?"

"There is no chupacabras. That was a story to keep the children away," Chef said. "Only Reaux doesn't understand children—a story like that will just make the little ones curious."

"That's for sure," Tom agreed, "especially boys!"

Chef explained more.

"As the children persisted Reaux had to try to convince them there really was a goatsucker here so he tried to scare them.

"The story did something else," he added. "It explained why no one saw Reaux out at night. He wasn't home, hiding from the chupacabras; he was out doing his dirty deeds."

"What a snake," said Antoinette.

Chef agreed, and then said to Tommy, "I hope you learned something about believing in all those stories little mon. You could have been hurt, or worse. From now on take these tall tales with a grain of salt."

"What does that mean?"

"That means to be skeptical my little friend. Ask questions. Don't believe everything you hear."

"I won't," Tommy said, "From now on I take it with a grain of salt."

"Good. Maybe your poor parents will get some rest," Chef said. "Maybe we'll all get some rest."

Then Chef's smile faded just a bit and he said, "And now my friends it is time for you to go."

Though they had all known it was time, this silenced both the children and adults. In the short time they had been there all had become close and comfortable friends. Having shared an adventure only made it that much better.

Finally, Judy took the initiative and began saying goodbye.

"Thank you all so much," she said.

"No," said Antoinette, "Thank you for the excitement. It finally woke this sleepy Chef up."

"But enough excitement," said Chef, "I want to get back to sleep."

Knowing it was time to get moving Tom sent the boys to load the luggage onto the empty carts. Peto went along to help.

As the adults finished saying their goodbyes the boys carried the bags from outside the cabanas to the cart. Picking the last bag from the ground Tyler suddenly stopped. He stooped to the ground and looked about *warily.*

"Peto," he said quietly, "Peto, look!"

On the ground was the jade medallion.

"I thought that was…" Peto started to say.

"So did I," said Tyler, picking it up.

Coming out of the cabana with Natalie, Paige immediately saw what was in Tyler's hand. Tyler stared up at his sister. Paige looked at the jade piece in Tyler's hand, then looked at Tyler and smiled.

"You know what this means," she said, "If Reaux didn't steal it and take it to town…"

"There may still be a chupacabras to be caught," said Tyler finishing Paige's thought.

They looked at the medallion lying in Tyler's palm wondering what to do with it.

"Come on you guys," Tom called.

Paige stood to answer him and Tyler turned to Peto. He handed him the medallion.

"Bait," he said, "for your next trap."

"No," said Peto, "I think this belongs in a museum. There is no chupa."

Tyler agreed.

"You're right Peto."

"Beside," Peto added, "I'm sure Reaux just dropped it when your brother hit him with coconut."

With that he stood, taking the last bag with him.

Soon they were rolling the luggage cart along. With their friends walking with them they headed to the dock and the waiting water taxis.

Suddenly Tommy turned and ran back toward the cabanas.

"Wait," he called over his shoulder, nearly tripping as he did. "I'll be right back."

As they all watched he ran first into one cabana then the other. When he came out he held coconut in his hand.

Running to catch up with them he held coconut up for all to see. On its wound was a bandage.

The End

What Is An Urban Legend?

Urban Legends are sensational stories that are repeated so often they come to be believed as true, even without any proof. These stories can be funny, frightening, or both. These stories spread quickly from person to person or via the Internet.

Many urban legends are retellings of old fashioned scary stories, such as The Vanishing Hitchhiker, a story of a hitchhiker who turns out to be a ghost. Others are based on existing tales or myths like the Jersey Devil, a devil-like creature alleged to live in the swamps and pine-barrens of New Jersey.

Still other urban legends are entirely new and are based on the changing world around us. An example of this is the story of Alligators in the Sewers. For some time it was believed that pet alligators that had been flushed down toilets when they were no longer wanted were thriving in the sewers of New York City. Not true.

What kind of urban legend is El Chupacabras?

Look for the next Oliver Family Adventure, Greenman, in spring 2005.

Glossary

Accomplice—Companion who helps another break the law.

Acquaintance—A casual friend, one known in passing.

Archeologist—A person who studies ancient times and peoples.

Aqui—(*Spanish*) Here; "In this place?"

Backwater—A forgotten or out of the way place.

Barbs—A sharp spine projecting backward making it difficult to remove.

Barracuda—A fierce, narrow-bodied tropical fish.

Barrier reef—A long ridge of coral near a coastline.

Bow—The front part of a ship or boat.

Bridge—The steering or command position of a boat or ship; usually above most of the vessel.

Cabana—A small building on the beach or by a pool.

Channel—The deepest part of a stream, river or harbor.

Claustrophobic—A frightening or uncomfortably confining space.

Contemplate—To think deeply about.

Cross—Showing a bad mood; annoyed.

Crest—A tuft or ridge on the head of a bird or animal.

Crystal Caves—Series of caverns near Kutztown, Pennsylvania. Discovered in 1871.

Deck—A platform from one side of a ship to the other; the floor of a ship or boat.

Discreetly—Modestly, secretly or tactfully; mindful of appearances.

Donde—(*Spanish*) Where, where?

Dreadlocks—A natural hairstyle in which the hair is twisted into long ropelike locks.

Dubbed—To give a name to playfully; nickname.

Elaborate—Intricate and rich in detail.

Encompassed—Indicated and included.

Esperar—(Spanish) To wait. "Wait!"

Estuary—The part of a river where its current is met by the sea.

Etchings—Picture or words scratched or scraped into something.

External—On the outside of something.

Façade—An artificial or deceptive front.

Flinch—To wince involuntarily, from surprise or pain.

Flotsam—Floating refuse or debris. Discarded odds and ends.

Foliage—Plant leaves, especially tree leaves.

Gingerly—Cautiously or carefully.

Grounding—To render a boat immobile by putting it partially on shore.

Haggle—To bargain over the price of something.

Hammock—A hanging bed suspended between two trees or other supports.

Hola—(*Spanish*) Hello.

Humble—Meek or modest; unpretentious; lowly. To make humble.

Inept—Bungling or clumsy; incompetent.

Intricate—Having many complex elements; elaborate.

Jade—Either of two distinct minerals, nephrite and jadeite, that are generally pale green or white and are used mainly as gemstones or in carving.

Key Island—One of a series of small, offshore islands.

Kelp—A brown, often very large seaweed.

Lagoon—A shallow body of water, especially one separated from a sea by sandbars or coral reefs.

Langosta—(*Spanish*) Lobster.

Lunge—A sudden forward movement, often threatening or attacking.

Manana—(*Spanish*) Tomorrow. "See you tomorrow."

Mangrove—Tropical tree growing near water, noted for its dramatic root system.

Marine—Aquatic, or of the sea.

Mollusks—Soft-bodied animals that live in a shell, such as clams, mussels and snails.

Myth—A traditional story dealing with supernatural beings, ancestors, or heroes.

Nada—(*Spanish*) Nothing.

Niche—A cranny, hollow, or crevice, as in rock.

Nocturnal—Most active at night.

Pantomime—Communication by means of gesture and facial expression.

Petrified—To be stunned or paralyzed with terror; dazed.

Plateau—A flat surface; especially, a broad, level, elevated area of land.

Plaza—A public square in a city or town.

Quarry—An open excavation or pit from which stone is obtained by digging or cutting.

Reservoir—A natural or artificial pond or lake used for the storage of water.

Rut—A sunken track or groove.

Sabotage—Action to defeat or hinder a cause or endeavor.

Sheath—A case for a knife or sword.

Stern—The back end of a ship or vessel.

Squall—A brief violent windstorm, often accompanied by rain or snow.

Taloned—Having talons or claws.

Taut—Pulled or drawn tight; not slack.

Thatch—Plant stalks or foliage, such as reeds or palm fronds, used for roofing.

Tourist—One who travels for pleasure.

Translate—To change into another language.

Trek—A long or trying journey.

Wake—The visible track or waves left by something moving through water: the wake of a ship.

Warily—Cautiously, with fear of harm.

Western Hemisphere—The half of the earth comprising North America, Central America, and South America.

Urban Legend—A story involving recent incidents that spreads quickly and is popularly believed to be true.

Winded—To be short of breath from activity.

0-595-33315-X

Printed in the United States
131988LV00001B/120/A